D1534852

On the Ropes

a Novella by

Hallee Bridgeman

Published by

Olivia Kimbrell Press™

Fort Knox, KY

i

On the Ropes by Hallee Bridgeman

Copyright © 2016. All rights reserved. No part of this publication may be reproduced or transmitted in any form or by any means electronic, mechanical, photocopying, or recording without express written permission of the author. The only exception is brief quotations in printed or broadcasted critical articles and reviews. This book is a work of fiction. Names, characters, places, and incidents are either the product of the author's imagination or are used fictitiously. Any resemblance to actual events, organizations, places, locales or to persons, living or dead, is purely coincidental and beyond the intent of either the author or publisher. The characters are productions of the author's imagination and used fictitiously.

PUBLISHED BY: Olivia Kimbrell Press*, P.O. Box 470, Fort Knox, KY 40121-0470. The Olivia Kimbrell Press™ colophon and open book logo are trademarks of Olivia Kimbrell Press™.

*Olivia Kimbrell Press™ is a publisher offering true to life, meaningful fiction from a Christian worldview intended to uplift the heart and engage the mind.

Some scripture quotations courtesy of the King James Version of the Holy Bible.

Some scripture quotations courtesy of the New King James Version of the Holy Bible, Copyright © 1979, 1980, 1982 by Thomas-Nelson, Inc. Used by permission. All rights reserved.

Original Cover Art by Amanda Gail Smith (amandagailstudio.com).

Library Cataloging Data

Names: Bridgeman, Hallee (Bridgeman Hallee) 1972-

Title: On the Ropes / Hallee Bridgeman

172 p. 5 in. × 8 in. (12.70 cm × 20.32 cm)

Description: Olivia Kimbrell Press™ digital eBook edition | Olivia Kimbrell Press™ Trade paperback edition | Kentucky: Olivia Kimbrell Press™, 2016.

Summary: Blow after blow, she hides her face and fights for her life.

Identifiers: LCCN: 2016911766 | ISBN-13: 978-1-68190-084-1 (hard cover) | 978-1-68190-035-3 (trade) | 978-1-68190-036-0 (POD) | 978-1-68190-034-6 (ebk.)

1. Christian social duties 2. courage confronting evil 3. sins of the father 4. witness protection 5. boxing fighting pugilism 6. mafia murder trail 7. special grand jury

---

ON THE ROPES

a Novella by

Table of Contents

Dedication

To everyone out there who has the courage to always do the right thing, even in the face of adversity.

Chapter 1

Present Day

Mara Harrison fanned her face with the ball cap, then took the end of her ponytail and wrapped her hair into a bun before settling the cap back on her head. The humidity and lack of breeze, coupled with the Florida summer sun beating down against the gravestones, made her feel like she'd spent the last hour working in a sauna. As she reached for her little shovel, she noted a faint pink tinge behind the freckles on her arm. With vibrant red hair, pale white skin, and freckles, she hardly had the complexion to work outside in the midday Florida summer. However, she had promised the pastor she would have the cemetery weeded by Friday, and she still had two sections to do.

"Time for a break, Mara," Pastor Ben Carmichael chided. He pushed the graveyard gate open with one hand while clutching two water bottles with the other. Despite the fact he'd spent the last two hours sitting on a riding lawn mower, he looked cool and crisp in his light blue golf shirt and khaki shorts. Even though his Florida Gators ball cap covered blond hair, his skin had tanned to a rich bronze since spring, while Mara's freckles provided the only color on her skin other than an occasional burn.

In the six months since Mara had relocated to the little village on the western coast of Florida, she and Ben had become good friends. The twenty-six-year-old pastor had bought the long-abandoned and dilapidated church they were working at with money inherited after the death of his grandfather. Over the last year, he had spent most waking moments restoring it and building the congregation.

Mara worked from home, doing medical transcription for four different doctors. That job gave her ample opportunity to volunteer during daylight hours at the church. She and Ben had lain carpet and tile, built shelves, planted bushes, weeded, and painted until she couldn't stand the thought of painting anymore. Under their love and care, the church bloomed, the congregation quadrupled in size, and Mara knew Ben's feelings for her had grown.

Part of her wanted to return his feelings, but a small part inside her held back. She knew she could never put him at risk. She didn't think she could live with herself if anything happened to him because of her. She also knew she could never enter into a romantic relationship predicated upon deception and misdirection.

Despite that, she liked him. A lot. Whenever he managed to get up the courage to profess his feelings for her, she hoped he wouldn't end their friendship over her rejection. She so desperately needed his friendship right now.

"Thanks," she smiled, accepting a water bottle from him, "it's hot out today."

"Too hot to be right out in it." He gestured at the sun directly overhead. "Why not stop for now and pick back up later this afternoon?"

She drained half the bottle before answering. "Can't. Have mandatory training about some changes in medical coding at three." She used her burning forearm to swipe at her damp forehead. "You have your first funeral here tomorrow. We need to get it finished."

He smiled at her, his brown eyes warm. "Had a feeling you'd say that." He gestured over his shoulder with his thumb. "That's why I rounded up some volunteers."

Three teenage boys from the youth group ambled into the cemetery. They all wore swim trunks and tank tops advertising a national fishing supply store. She knew the tallest boy, Jeremy, had a pool and guessed they'd spent the morning there before coming to work at the church. "Hi, boys," Mara said with a smile as Ben headed back to his mower, "ready to get to work?"

"Yes, ma'am," Jeremy replied, always the outspoken one of the group. "Mama said we had to spend four hours here, and you'd give us the Wi-Fi code she texted pastor this morning."

"We tried going to our house," one of the two Cantrell brothers said, "but Jeremy's mom had already conspired with our mom."

Mara laughed. "The Bible says to serve God with a willing heart."

The youngest of the three grimaced. "We're willing, ma'am."

Mara showed them the section of the graveyard to weed and gave them a wheelbarrow and tools. Once she saw they had it under control, she doused herself with more sunscreen, traded the ball cap for a floppy wide-brimmed straw hat, and went back to attacking the weeds covering the hundred-year-old grave of, according to the inscription on the stone, a beloved grandmother. The new hat offered much more protection from the sun, and the bottle of water she'd consumed helped energize her. Letting her mind wander, she found herself thinking about what the air would feel like a thousand miles away in Manhattan right about now.

"Mara!"

The panic in the boy's tone pushed every other thought from her mind. One of the brothers rushed toward her. "A snake bit Jeremy!"

Heart pounding, she rushed to where she'd left the boys working. She found Jeremy sitting on the ground, staring at the still twitching body of the headless rattlesnake. One of the boys had killed it with a hoe. The snake looked enormous—five feet long, at least.

Despite the six-month hiatus, her medical training took over. She retrieved her pocket knife as she crouched next to Jeremy. He sat on the pine straw-covered ground, clutching his right hand with his left. "Is that where it bit you?" He looked dazed. "Move your hand," she ordered, "let me see."

Taking his hand in hers, she lowered it closer to the ground to get the bite below his heart. "My shin, too," he panted. Inspecting his face, she witnessed his pupils dilate. His breathing came short and quick. Looking at his calf, she saw the other bite. "Which first?"

"Hand," he said on a breath.

"Call 9-1-1," she ordered the youngest Cantrell, "and go get Pastor Ben." She touched his cheek to get his attention. "Listen, Jeremy, I need you to calm down. We're going to move you to this bench right here." She helped him up then settled him on the stone bench. "Keep your hand down. Below your heart." She inspected the wounds and checked his vital signs, wishing she had a blood pressure cuff.

She looked up at the older Cantrell boy. "EMTs on the way?"

"Yes, ma'am," he confirmed.

Ben and the younger brother rushed onto the scene. "What happened?"

"Two rattlesnake bites." As she spoke, Jeremy turned his body away from her and vomited into the grass behind the bench. "Jeremy, that's just the venom making you sick. Try to take slow deep breaths. We need to try to keep your heart rate down." She pressed her fingers to the jugular on his neck, then double-checked the distal pulse at his wrist, looking for a discrepancy. Two minutes had passed. With every heartbeat, the venom moved further into his body. She couldn't wait any longer. "Give me your shirt," she said to the youngest brother. He slipped it over his head and held it out to her. "I need two sticks," she said to no one in particular. "About six inches long. Strong. Hurry!"

Pulling out her pocketknife, she cut the tank top in half. She tied half of it right below Jeremy's elbow in a surgeon's knot, and the other half right above his knee. "Where're my sticks?"

"Will these work?" Ben asked, offering four oak twigs about half an inch in diameter.

She snatched them with a nod. Picking up the running ends of the tourniquet below his elbow, she tied a square knot on top of the stick, trapping it between the square knot and the surgeon's knot. Then she twisted the stick like turning a spigot, tightening the makeshift tourniquet until as much of the venom as possible remained trapped below his elbow, away from his heart. Finally, she secured the stick in place with the ends of the shirt.

Using another stick, she repeated the process above his knee; the wound furthest from his heart and the snake's second strike, making it the lower priority. Jeremy moaned. "I know it hurts," she agreed, her heart aching a bit at causing him so much pain, "but you're tough, and I hear the ambulance."

As sirens sounded in the distance, she checked the tightness of the tourniquets and checked his pulse in his neck and wrist again. The flesh around the fang marks on his hand had gone from red to a purplish black. The venom had already started to denature the protein in his flesh.

"What can I do?" Ben asked.

She swiped at her forehead with her forearm. "Pray."

Three Years Ago

Ruth Burnette stood on the corner of the street and stared at the coffee shop. Her twin sister, Esther, slipped an arm over her shoulders. "You're doing it today, right?"

She looked over at her mirror image, her best friend, her partner in crime. Esther had her bronze hair pulled back into a braid that fell down the back of her blue silk blouse. They both had graduated from Columbia Medical School six months ago. While Esther pursued a career as a psychiatrist, Ruth had chosen to specialize in thoracic surgery. She looked at her watch. Rounds started in twenty minutes. "I'm out of time."

"You are not. Get your rear in there and talk to him, or I'll go pretend I'm you."

With a gasp, Ruth said, "You would not!"

"Don't test me." Despite sounding so firm, her twin's mouth twitched in a smile. "Now, go. I'm right beside you."

Nervous energy made her hand flutter to her stomach, but she lifted her chin and marched into the coffee shop. As she opened the door, the smell of fresh ground beans made her mouth water. A line of people stretched from the counter, waiting to place orders, while a crowd milled around the other side, where they would pick up their order fulfillments. Scanning all the faces, disappointment overtook her nervousness. "He's not here."

"He's been here every day for over a month. Of course, he's here."

They made their way to the line. Ruth rechecked her

watch. She couldn't afford to be late for rounds. She may have to skip coffee this morning.

"Hello."

At the sound of his voice, her heart lurched in her chest. Turning, she spied Victor Kovalev standing behind her in the line. He must have entered the shop right behind her. He wasn't much taller than her five-seven, with a lean build and dark hair that almost curled. Normally, she found herself getting lost in his rich brown eyes, but today, the purpling bruise and swollen left eye made her gasp. "What happened?"

"Wha—?" He stopped mid-word, and gingerly touched his upper cheek. She could see the swollen bruising on his knuckles. "Oh, that. I had a fight last night."

"You got into a fight?" Esther asked frowning.

His eyebrows knit in a confused look, then he pulled the sports section from *The Times* out of his bag. On the front page, a color photo of a boxer in royal blue and bright red shorts punched another boxer wearing yellow and black shorts. Upon closer examination, she recognized Victor as the boxer in blue and red. "This is you?"

"It is." He smiled a closed-lip smile and took the paper back from her as a faint tinge of red covered his cheeks. "I thought you knew."

"I don't know much about boxing." Despite social expectancies and personal space, despite the nervousness at even speaking to him this morning, the doctor in her took over, and she took his chin in one hand and carefully but skillfully palpitated the area around his eye with her fingers. "Has a doctor seen this?"

He stood perfectly still while she examined him but grinned at her with a smile that had started to bare straight white teeth. His smile made her heart skip a beat. "Yes, ma'am. She just did."

Flustered, she stepped away and gave her order at the counter. As soon as Esther and Victor ordered, they joined the throng waiting for their drinks. Esther gently nudged her and nodded toward Victor. Before she could talk herself out of it, she blurted, "Would you like to go to church with me tonight?"

They always met at this coffee shop, the one where they originally ran into each other, every morning at 6:30. She realized after the third meeting that he intentionally came to meet her, and very quickly started to look forward to it. He'd asked her out daily for about six weeks. Because her residency schedule proved so grueling, she had turned him down, but she always found time for church, and she so wanted to get to know him better.

"Church?" His smile started to fade, and his eyebrows lowered suspiciously.

Her stomach fell. He looked so taken aback, so confused. What had she done? "You have an objection to church?"

"I don't know." Instantly, his face transformed back into a grin that lit up the whole room. "Why don't we find out? What time?"

Chapter 2

Present Day

Mara sat in an orange plastic chair in the hospital's waiting room, wishing she had a light sweater to combat the artificially cool air. Hours had passed. Anxiety at not knowing Jeremy's condition, coupled with her intellectual knowledge of how bad it might actually be, made her feel like she could jump out of her skin at any moment. Instead, she sat perfectly still, occasionally allowing her lips to move with a silent prayer.

About every five minutes, she stopped herself from going to the nurse behind the desk and asking for updates. Knowing how the emergency room system worked, that nurse wouldn't know anything and would just send her back to her chair to wait some more. The nurse had her own job to do and didn't need a restless woman hounding her constantly.

The familiar sounds and smells gave Mara a pang of homesickness that brought tears to her eyes. It would do no good to cry about it. She'd cried all the tears she would allow herself to cry months before. This part of her life, the organized chaotic efficiency of an emergency room, no longer existed for her.

The double doors leading to the back swung open, and Ben walked through them. Surging to her feet, she stopped herself from rushing toward him and slipped her hands into the pockets of her shorts, clenching them into fists. Ben looked tired. That couldn't be good.

"He's going to live," he said immediately, clearly reading the anxiety on her face or possibly in her body language. "Thanks to you."

She started to shrug but caught herself. "That snake was so big. I knew the bites were bad."

He nodded. "Doc said if you hadn't have done what you did, things would have gone a lot worse." He pulled his car keys out of his pocket. "Ready to go?" She looked at the double doors. No, she was not ready to go. She did not want to leave. Instead, she wanted to go back there and read his chart, confer with the doctors, and make sure they'd put the best course of action into play. She wanted to check on her patient, scribble notes to the nurses, and reassure the parents.

Instead, she smiled and said, "Sure." He put a hand on the small of her back and led her to the parking lot. With the sun all but gone, she expected the night air to have some chill to it, but instead of cool evening air, she stepped into muggy heat.

Settled into the passenger seat of Ben's car, with the air conditioning blowing in her face, she looked out the window and out into the darkness beyond the parking lot. "Where did you learn to do that to a snake bite?"

She bit her tongue on the words "Columbia Pre-Med" and instead said, "John Wayne." She glanced at him and saw his jaw tighten, knowing he resented that she'd sidestepped yet another question. "Ben—"

"No." He visibly relaxed and stole a glance at her. "It doesn't matter." He looked back at the road. "When you're ready, I'm here."

Ready for what? To spill the ugly truth? If she asked that he'd likely press for answers. Answers she would never give. Not in this lifetime. Instead, she looked back out the window and rode the rest of the way home in silence.

Three Years Ago

Victor walked into the gym. Even at seven in the morning, men filled the facility, utilizing workout machines or punching bags, or sparring in one of the three rings. The collective sound, while chaotic, comforted him. In the early morning, the gym still smelled faintly of pine. In twelve hours, the place would smell like feet and corn chips. Even those smells comforted him, just like the dim lighting and the sweat-soaked air. His family owned gyms all over the borough. Among a massive family empire and various business interests, they sponsored boxers and mixed martial arts fighters. His uncle Boris managed a lot of the fighters, including Victor himself. At 27 and with three championship wins, he neared retirement. He knew that once that happened, his time in the gym would be spent upstairs where his father had his main office that smelled faintly of old tobacco and muffled the noise of the gym. For now, though, he stayed downstairs, in his territory, among the blood, sweat, tears, and tape.

"Yo, Vic!"

He glanced up into the ring and saw his trainer, Joe, tying the gloves onto Anthony, one of the company's newest and most favored to replace him as he approached the end of his career. He lifted his hand in a greeting.

"Great fight last night!" Anthony said as Joe stepped back, and he shadowboxed a couple left jabs.

"Thanks, man."

"You want to join me?"

He laughed and shook his head, pointing to the bruised eye. "Always take the day off after a fight, Anthony. Secret to my success. I'm going to drop off this uniform and maybe go feed pigeons in the park."

"Pigeons?" Anthony rested his gloved hands on the top rope and leaned forward. "You afraid to fight me, old man?"

He felt his neck bristle with the challenge even as he saw the teasing gleam in Anthony's eye. He held both hands up as if in surrender. "Yeah. You caught me. The weight of my championship belts would probably slow me down in the ring boxing you and your title-less self." He waved in his direction. "See you tomorrow. Bet you won't be so quick to challenge me then."

Joe, an old boxing champ from 1977, pointed at him. "Victor. Get your eye checked out. By a doctor. Do that before you do anything else today. Clear?"

Thinking of honey brown eyes and hair the color of the most beautiful sunsets, he saluted his trainer. "Already saw a doc this morning." He walked past the ring, spinning around to face Joe. "She wants to see me again. No worries."

As he went to his locker and unpacked his bag, replacing the items with clean clothes and filling a laundry bag with dirty items, he thought back to his encounter with Ruth that morning. It had shocked him when she had invited him to church. No one had ever done that before. He'd go through almost anything, though, to see her, including this elusive thing called church. He paused and frowned as he shoved a pair of socks into the laundry bag. He had no business pursuing her, all things considered. Why was he doing this?

He had a destiny sitting upstairs, a destiny that involved taking over his father's empire. For now, boxing took up all his time. Everyone knew that once he retired, he'd take his place at his father's right hand, and Ruth Burnette certainly had no business next to him there. Of course, he didn't have to retire just yet. He could box a couple more years, buy a little more time.

He remembered the first time he met Doctor Ruth Burnette in that coffee shop. She'd turned and looked up at him, her eyes wide with shock and embarrassment over their collision, and he'd momentarily been stunned into immobility. She had long curly hair, the color of the richest sunsets streaked with orange and red and gold. He wanted to touch it, to feel the warmth he just knew it radiated. Her pale brown eyes, the same color as the freckles scattered across her porcelain skin, shone with an inner light of life and happiness. He'd realized he was staring when he saw her lips moving, but could hear nothing besides a buzzing sound in his ears.

Shaking his head, he slammed the locker shut. He'd go to church. Maybe it would be the most awful thing in the world, and all this concern for the future would dissipate by evening's end. He carried the laundry bag to the cart in the corner of the room and tossed it in there. One of the girls would see to the laundering and return of his items. Instead of walking back through the gym, he pushed the door to the alley open and stepped out into the cold January morning. As he walked toward the street, a snowflake fell and hovered in front of his face, dancing away from him in a swirl of icy wind. He suddenly realized he hoped church wouldn't be the worst thing in the world.

Chapter 3

Present Day

Mara set her newspaper down and took a sip of her iced coffee. The sun had barely crested the top of the pine trees, and already the day promised more heat and humidity than the day before. She'd grown to enjoy the weather in her time here. She smiled as her friend, Kelly Jamison, stepped onto her porch. Mara could always count on Kelly to share the early morning hours with her. "You're famous," Kelly announced.

Her heart skipped a beat, and her hand paused on the head of her German shepherd, Major. "Famous?"

Kelly handed Mara her phone. "Look. You're all over Friendspace." Mara looked at the screen and saw a series of photos from the day before, of her treating and tending to Jeremy. Most of the pictures just showed the back of her head, but on one of them, she could clearly see her face. Below the photos, she saw hundreds of social media shares. Panic skirted up her back. Major's ears perked, and he looked at her face as if trying to decide whether he should go on alert.

"I have to go," she said, lunging to her feet. "I just made that pot of coffee in there. Help yourself." She opened the door and let Major into the cottage, then ran down the steps and on down the street. Three blocks away, she rushed through the gate into the yard of a large home. As she bounded up the stairs to the long porch, the door opened, and Jeremy's mother, Brenda, stepped out, purse over her arm.

"Well," she said, clearly startled, "I was on my way to the hospital but was going to stop by and see you."

"How's Jeremy?" Mara asked, straining with the need to say what she really came to say.

"The doctor said if you hadn't acted so quickly with the tourniquets, he wouldn't be here today. I owe you my son's life. Thank you."

"I'm just glad I was there. I feel bad since he was helping me." As casually as possible, she said, "Listen, Brenda, I wanted to ask you a favor."

"Anything," the older woman said passionately.

"Those pictures you posted...." She cleared her throat. "Could you possibly delete the one where you can see my face?"

Brenda raised an eyebrow. "Mara?"

"I just—" she stopped as her voice cracked, and uninvited tears burned her eyes. "I came here to get away from a guy. I don't have a phone, and I don't have Friendspace. I'm trying to lay low until he quits, you know, trying to find me." She only skirted the truth. She looked over her shoulder as if expecting someone to sneak up behind her, then back at Brenda. "I've never said anything, and I appreciate you keeping it to yourself. It's important."

Brenda pulled out her phone, and seconds later said, "Done." Mara felt a tightening in her heart loosen. As she slipped her phone back into her purse, she said, "One of the Cantrell boys took the pictures, but I'm the one who posted them. You might want to get with him." She reached out and put her hand on Mara's arm. "If you ever need anything, anything at all, you come here. You hear?"

"Yes, ma'am." Before she could think about it, she let Brenda pull her into a hug. The tears slid down her cheeks. "Please, don't tell anyone. I'd hate to be the subject of gossip."

"Tell anyone what?" Brenda said with a smile that promised all was already forgotten. She put her hands on Mara's shoulders. "Thank you again."

Two Years Ago

Ruth rushed through her apartment. As she entered her room, she kicked off her shoes and whipped her shirt over her head. She wouldn't even bother changing, except that three hours ago, on her way out of the hospital, already dressed for her evening with Victor and his parents, a stream of ambulances arrived carrying multiple victims from a massive car accident in the Lincoln Tunnel.

By the time she'd managed to leave the emergency

room, she discovered bloodstains on her shoes and shirt. A quick text to Victor begging for an extra thirty minutes bought her enough time to rush home, but just. A terrible rainstorm pummeled the city and made the commute home take twice as long as it should have. Only through the grace of the Lord above would she be able to get showered and changed in time before Victor arrived to pick her up.

Shutting the bathroom door behind her, she heard her apartment door open. "It's just me!" Esther singsonged. "I have a surprise for you!"

"I'll be out in a minute," Ruth yelled through the door. "Victor will be here any sec. Can you listen for him?"

For almost a year, Victor had spent most of Ruth's available time in her apartment. He preferred to stay in rather than go out. What outings they did take usually involved church or their young adult church group.

Early in their relationship, he invited her to one of his cousin's nightclubs, but she'd turned him down. He'd seemed relieved about her declining the invitation, and because of her grueling work schedule, his desire to stay in completely appealed to her. In fact, when he asked her to come to dinner at his parents' house tonight, it had taken her completely by surprise. She had never met his parents. Since her own parents died when she and Esther were nineteen, the whole meeting parents thing never even occurred to her.

Deciding against washing her hair then drying it just to have to step outside in the rain, she threw it into a braid and quickly put on a skirt and blouse. Rain boots, a cute scarf, and a smudge of lipstick, and she was ready just as she heard a knock on the door. When she opened her bedroom door, the pitiful little bark made her stop.

Esther bent down and scooped up the puppy. "Meet Major," she grinned. "I found him under a mailbox on Fifth."

The little German shepherd whined and nuzzled his nose into Esther's neck. He couldn't have been more than two or three months old. "Oh," she exclaimed, her heart breaking into a million pieces then coming back together entirely in love. She ran a finger over his damp head. "What a sweetie."

She rushed to the door when she heard another knock, throwing it open and grinning at Victor. "Hi!"

With his strong Slavic features and wearing black jeans and a black turtleneck with a black leather jacket, he looked decidedly eastern European. A warm kiss from him weakened her knees. He smelled of rain, leather, and aftershave. She stepped back away from him and ran a hand down the lapel of his jacket, then gestured so that he would come in. "Thanks for the extra time. There was an emergency."

"Yeah. I saw on the news." He slipped his hands into the pockets of his jacket. "I have a cab waiting. I thought it would be better than trying to navigate the train and walking in the rain."

"Great idea." She grabbed her purse from the back of the couch and walked over to Esther. "This is our new family member, Major," she said, scooping the puppy from her sister's arms. "Isn't he the sweetest thing?"

If she hadn't already been hopelessly in love with the

Russian boxer in front of her, the way his face softened when he scrubbed a finger under the chin of the puppy certainly would have been the catalyst. "Hello there, Major," he murmured. "You look so scared."

"He was cowering under a mailbox in this storm. My heart just broke for him." Esther took the puppy from Ruth and waved at the door. "Don't leave your cab waiting. They're probably hard to get tonight, with this weather. I'm going to see what I can do to get this little one settled in."

She heard Esther lock the door behind them and slipped her hand into Victor's as they walked to the elevator. He pulled her close as the doors slid shut. With her head resting on his shoulder, she just breathed him in.

"Nervous?" he asked.

"I was." She straightened as the ground floor approached and slipped on her jacket. "Then I had to talk to the mother of a sixteen-year-old and explain the radical amputation they're doing to her son's leg. Suddenly, meeting your parents became something to look forward to rather than fear."

As they stepped out of the elevator, he pulled her over to the side and cupped her face with his hands. His eyes burned with intensity, and a serious expression crossed his face. "I love you," he said, his voice hoarse.

He'd said it to her a dozen times in the past week, and she still felt her heart soar a little higher every time he said the words. "I love you, too."

His kiss spoke of love, of promises to come, and, dare she hope, a long future together. She felt tears burn her eyes as the love she felt for this man overwhelmed her and spilled out of her. When he lifted his head, he smiled down at her. "Can I tell you something?"

"Anything."

"Major is the worst name for a dog I've ever heard in my entire life."

She giggled and slipped her hand in his again as they walked through the lobby of her apartment building. "You never know with Esther what made her choose that name. If I had time tonight, I would have gotten the story out of her." The doorman opened the door, and she smiled at him as they rushed to the waiting cab. Brushing the water out of her braid, she laughed, "I'm glad I didn't spend any time on my hair."

He gave his parents' address to the cab driver, then settled back in the seat, Ruth snuggling up to his side. "You look beautiful." She could hear his heartbeat under her ears, smell him, feel his warmth. She thought that if she could stay in this position for the rest of her life, she would be absolutely content. "Listen, my father—"

When he paused, she lifted her head to look at him. "What?"

"He's, uh, very hard. A hard man. He comes from old school Russia. He might not treat you very nice. But you must understand this is just the man he is."

Wanting to put him at ease, she put her hand on his cheek and laughed. "I'm a second-year surgical resident. I'm used to people not being nice to me." She gave him a quick peck of a kiss, then settled back against the seat. "Don't worry. You've managed to make me fall in love with you over the last year. Your father could be a mass murderer, and it wouldn't affect my feelings for you." She looked over at him, at the lack of humor on his face, and winked. "Well played, Kovalev, waiting until now to introduce me to him. You have me well and captured."

He cleared his throat and pulled her closer. "Just don't let him—"

"Quit worrying!" She now understood the reason he hadn't introduced her to his parents before now. Clearly, he feared his father would somehow negatively affect her feelings for him. As well as she knew him, as much time as they had spent together in the last several months, she knew nothing could ever take away her love for him.

Chapter 4

Present Day

Victor Kovalev walked through the gym, looking at the two men sparring in the boxing ring. He recognized the taller one by the tattoo of Moscow's Red Square covering his entire back. He didn't like sparring with him in the ring—he tended to fight dirty. The way his opponent kept shielding his face, he wondered what maliciousness the man had been up to during this particular practice fight.

In years past, he would have stopped at the ring and chatted with the trainers and fighters. Now, they glanced at him in his navy suit and leather shoes, then looked past him like he wasn't even there. He ducked into the office and nodded at his uncle Boris, who listened on his phone, a cigarette hanging out of the corner of his mouth. He'd shed his standard black leather coat and openly wore a shoulder harness with two customized wooden-handled Tokarev TT-30s in each holster. He had carved some notches into one of the handles.

Next to him, his son, Marco, sat in front of two laptops, typing on one, looking at another. By the back door, a blonde woman in a leather miniskirt sat on a wooden chair, her head thrown back, eyes open, staring off in a drugged haze.

Marco looked at Victor, spoke in Russian very softly, and then hung up the phone. "Well. If it isn't the crown prince himself come to mingle with the peasants and the *kulaks*. What can I do for you, Victor?" Boris asked, squinting at him through the smoke.

Victor held up the envelope in his hand. "I got subpoenaed by the state to testify at father's trial."

Boris took a long drag of his cigarette and ground it out in the ashtray. When he spoke, smoke came out of his nose and mouth. "Why would they need your testimony? They already have your loud-mouthed girlfriend, and her eye-witness account is supposed to be so very damning, is that not so?"

Heaving a sigh, he kept his voice flat and said, "She is not my girlfriend."

"No," his uncle replied, standing and walking around the desk. He stopped when his toes touched Victor's, so close to him, their noses almost touched. His nose filled with the odor of cigarette smoke and sweat, "But it was because she once was your girl that your father is now sitting in prison, waiting for trial. You made this mess. You." At the last "you," Boris dug a finger into Victor's chest, and Victor held his breath in defense against the offensive odors. He didn't wince. They'd had this same conversation every time they had met in person for six months. He grew tired of Boris' accusations after the first day. "Tell me, Victor. How do they even know you were there, eh?"

"Clearly, someone mouthed off." He pushed Boris's hand away and waved the paper at him. "I don't know why they subpoenaed me. What do you think I should do? Huh?" Raising his voice, getting intentionally loud and defensive, he added, "Scamper away to the motherland and hide until all of the trial is over? You know as well as I do that papka can beat this. Our sources have all said that her testimony is weak because of the rain that night."

Boris ran his hands over his thinning, greased back hair, and nodded, stepping away from Victor. "You're right. Reasonable doubt. That's how they do things here."

"We don't have anything to worry about, uncle."

"No, but when we find that girlfriend of yours, she'll know what it means to worry." He gestured to the man sitting at the computer. "Marco finally hacked the TSA system last night. He's preparing a program to run facial recognition software. We'll be able to spot her the second she steps into a terminal in New York."

Victor met Marco's eyes. His cousin smiled a rather feral smile, showing off his gold front tooth.

"With the security she'll likely be under, why risk it if her testimony isn't supposed to be reliable in the first place?"

"To send a message," Boris said as he squinted at his phone screen and dialed a number. "Apparently, her sister's untimely death didn't teach her a clear enough lesson. No one can threaten the Kovalevs." He turned his back on Victor and spoke rapid Russian into the phone, clearly dismissing his nephew.

Victor looked at his cousin. "How does that work?"

"It accesses all of the cameras in the city," Marco said, turning a screen to point at a grid of a dozen camera angles. "When the program finds her face, it will track her from camera to camera until we know where she is staying."

Knowing how brilliant Marco was with programming, Victor didn't doubt for a second that what he said the program could do, it would do. "What if she has a hat or a wig or something? Or if she had plastic surgery?"

Marco turned the screen back toward himself and went back to typing on the other laptop. "It's not a perfect plan, but right now, we don't know where she is at all, so it's better than nothing." He gestured at one of the screens. "I have the same facial recognition scanning social media and news sites. It's possible we find her before she even comes to the trial next week."

Boris ended his call and walked over to the girl sitting in the chair, kicking at her legs and jarring her out of her stupor. "You have a client," he said, handing her a piece of paper. "Remy will drive you."

Victor watched as the look of disgust and fear crossed her face when she saw the address, but she did not argue. She stood to her feet, looking rather wobbly, and teetered a bit on her four-inch heels. Slipping her purse strap over her shoulder, she left the office, casting a glance at Victor as she brushed by him.

Six Months Ago

"You would have more energy if you would eat something other than this," Victor said, pushing his finger against the foil-wrapped hamburger. "I would think that as a medical professional, you'd know better." He uncapped his pen and started writing in his notebook, preparing for a testimony their pastor had asked him to give that Sunday. At his elbow, his Bible sat open. Ruth wanted to ask him what he planned to speak on, but she knew he'd tell her to wait until Sunday.

"I'm a poor resident," she replied, scooping up the burger and unwrapping it. Before she took a bite, she grinned at him, sitting rather uncomfortably in the orange plastic chair. "It's what I can afford."

He pressed his lips together and shook his head, making her laugh around her bite of food. The tangy pickle added a crunch to the bite loaded with savory hamburger topped with mayonnaise and ketchup. She had always thought the flavor combination one of the most perfect tastes in the world. It helped that she'd not eaten since dinner last night. Her hand shook a bit from hunger as she dipped a French fry in the ketchup.

He took a sip from his bottle of water. "I think a plate of rice and beans would offer so much more nutrition than that hamburger and cost a fraction of the price."

"You need to be more adventurous in your food," she proclaimed around a second bite. "In moderation, occasional fast food won't kill you."

"This is true. Occasionally." He raised an eyebrow. "How much fast food have you eaten this week?"

"Be nice." She took another bite and washed it down with her iced tea. "I'm trying to get a handle on my schedule so I can prepare meals before going to the hospital, but these hours are killing me. If I survive this residency, I'll deserve a medal."

He winked charmingly, making her heart flip with love for him. "I'll give you one of my championship belts."

She stared at him as she chewed a fry. He had taken a hard hit in his last match, and she didn't like how long it had taken him to recover. "How are you feeling about Saturday's fight?"

The hesitation he gave in answering her question answered her more than his words. "Fighting the last fight of my career in Madison Square Garden on New Year's Eve? Honestly, I couldn't have asked for a better exit." Despite the words, his voice sounded unenthusiastic, almost bored.

With narrowed eyes, she tried to study his pupils. "You in fighting shape?"

Victor shrugged. "He is a brawler. I plan to stick and move for the first few rounds, then keep him on the ropes when he gets tired."

"You avoided my question. Are you in shape?"

As a grimace crossed his face, he set his pen down and closed his notebook. She thought maybe she should have kept that thought to herself. He looked at her with a long, studying look. Just when she opened her mouth to withdraw the question, he reached out and took her hand with his. "I have a question for you. Will you marry me?"

Her mouth fell open. They'd talked about this six months ago, but she'd asked him to wait for another year. She wanted to finish her surgical residency before they got married. So many details would go into planning a wedding, and she wanted to have the freedom to focus on those details rather than work. "You know I will. Just give me another six months."

Reaching into his backpack, he pulled out the jewelry box that contained her ring. "I don't want to wait six months or a year," he said, setting the box in front of them and taking her hand in both his. Passionately, he leaned forward. "I don't want to wait another minute. Let's go get married and go away from the city. You can transfer your residency, right?"

Her eyebrows came together in a frown. "What are you talking about? Why would we leave the city?"

For a moment, he stared at her with such intensity it took her breath away. Then his face relaxed, and he sat back, letting go of her hand and slipping the ring back into his bag. "Nothing. Forget I said anything." He scooped his Bible and notebook into his bag and zipped it shut. Ruth just sat there, staring at him, unsure of what just happened. "I have to go. I'm meeting Joe at the gym in an hour, and I know you have to get back to the hospital." He slipped out of his chair. As he walked by her, he put a hand on her shoulder. "I'll see you tomorrow. Breakfast at your place, right?"

"Right," she whispered as he left. She stared at her leftover dinner, no longer hungry, worried about what had just happened. She put her leftover food on the tray and dumped it into the trashcan by the door. The whole way back to the hospital, she thought about it. For a few moments, Victor had seemed almost frightened. Why would he want to leave the city? Why would he ask her to give up all that she had worked for here just to have to start over somewhere else? Did he not know what life was like for her behind the scenes in the hospital? She had one of the most sought-after surgical residency positions in the state. Surely, he knew that. And unlike him, who would retire from his career this weekend, she had just started hers. Nothing about moving would hold any kind of reason right now.

Something made him scared. She was sure of it. What could it be?

By the time she made it to the locker room, worry fully occupied her mind. What was wrong? What had spurred that whole conversation?

"Doctor Friedman is looking for you," her friend, Jane, said, opening the locker next to hers. "He said you were to get some lab work for him that he needs in an hour."

"I did it," she said absently, touching the sleeve of her white coat hanging in the locker, but not putting it on. "The lab texted me five minutes ago." She watched as Jane slipped out of her own coat and pulled a sweatshirt out of her locker. "Are you off?"

Jane grinned, pulling the sweatshirt over her head. "I am. I have some of my Aunt May's leftover Christmas pecan pie sitting in my fridge with my name on it."

Plunging forward, she shut her locker and stepped

closer to her friend. "Can you take the rest of my shift for me?"

Clearly, the urgency in her heart translated to her face and voice because Jane immediately put her hands on her shoulders. "What's wrong?"

"I don't know," Ruth said, shaking her head, "but I need to go find out. Please. I'll work New Year's Day for you."

Jane narrowed her eyes, as if in contemplation, then nodded. "And the night before."

"After Vic's fight. I'll come straight here."

"Deal." Jane grinned and whipped the sweatshirt back off. "What patient are those labs for?"

An hour later, after briefing Jane on all her patients, she went to her apartment. Major and Esther were not home yet. She took a long shower, changed into fresh clothes, and slipped back out of the apartment. Victor said he had training with Joe. She knew Joe mainly worked at the main gym. Halfway there, it started raining, and she could see streaks of sleet in the rain illuminated by the streetlights. Shivering a bit in the cold, she pulled her umbrella out of her bag and kept walking, bending into the driving rain, using the umbrella almost like a shield. Finally, she made it to the gym.

The closed sign made her frown. She knew this place stayed open until eleven most nights. Why would it say closed? Maybe since Victor was training for such a big fight, they closed the gym so he could train in private.

She tried the door anyway, almost surprised when it opened. Bright fluorescent lights lit the room, shining on the mats and pads. Mirrors along the walls reflected everything back at her. The smell of stale sweat mixed with antiseptic and leather eased into her nostrils. Usually, the gym was full of men working out, sparring in the rings, or lifting weights. Tonight, she saw no one. She heard no clangs of weights, no voices sparring, no music playing, but dirty towels lined the mats, and she saw a couple of gym bags, including Victor's, by the ring. It looked as if everyone had left in a hurry.

She heard a voice from the back of the gym. Looking all around, she walked through the large room. As she turned a corner, she jumped a bit, startled when her peripheral vision caught her own reflection in a mirror. Heart pounding, every sense heightened, she put her hand to her chest and took a deep breath. This sudden terror didn't have a place here, in Victor's family's realm. She couldn't understand why she felt so nervous.

She heard the sound of a man's voice again. Continuing through the building, she passed the open door of Victor's uncle Boris' office. Knowing he managed the fighters, arranged the fights, and worked with the promotions of the fights, she hoped to find Victor and his team in there, talking about the upcoming match.

She peered into the office but saw no one. Several hundred-dollar bills lay scattered on the floor, and a chair lay overturned near the back door. Turning another corner, she saw the door to the alley propped open and heard a voice even through the sound of the driving rain. As she walked closer, she realized the man spoke in Russian. Hoping she'd find Victor out there, she put her hand on the door and pushed it open.

In the dim light of the alley, through the rain, she saw three men on their knees in front of Antoly Kovalev, Victor's father. She froze. Part of her brain realized the extent of what she saw. Another part of her brain completely rejected the image. Two of the men had their heads bowed, hands behind their backs. Streams of water from the rain ran down their heads to the ground. The middle man had his head raised, his hands folded in front of him as if praying. She couldn't tell if tears streamed down his face or if it was rain. A man she did not know walked up behind that man and put a gun to the base of his skull.

The sound of the gunshot made her whole body jump. She immediately clasped both hands to her mouth to block the scream lodged in her throat. As the man fell forward, the other two men raised their heads and started talking rapidly in Russian, but both of them met the same fate as their companion.

Eyes wide, heart pounding so hard she could hear it through the roaring in her ears, she slowly stepped backward. She moved out of the door's path, and it slammed shut, knocking the doorstop away. Through the window glass laced with a net of wire, she saw Antoly raise his head and stare right at her. His eyes narrowed, and she saw his mouth move.

Run, she told herself. Run! On shaking knees, she turned and scrambled through the gym, sprinting, arms pumping. She burst through the main doors and onto the sidewalk. Frantic, she looked around. Which way to go? As she spun, her feet slipped, and she stumbled forward into the road. Bright lights and blaring horns made it hard to focus. Her hands came down on the hood of a cab. Keeping her hands on the hood, as if she had the power to hold it in place, she rushed to the door and opened it.

The cabbie did not even look surprised by her appearance. "Drive!" she yelled as the man with the gun came out of the alley. "Go!"

They sped past the man just as Antoly emerged from the alley. She looked through the back glass as the cab turned and merged into the traffic on Fifth Avenue.

Chapter 5

Present Day

Mara woke with a start. Heart pounding, she held her breath. Had she heard a sound in real life or in her dream? *Calm down, Mara.* As her eyes adjusted to the dark, she spotted Major asleep on his bed under the window. If the noise had actually occurred outside her dream, he would have sounded the alarm. Forcing herself to lie back down, she steadied her breathing and tried to close her eyes, but she immediately saw the men on their knees through the curtain of sleet, heard the sound of the gun going off, heard the desperate cries from one of the other men.

Tears streaming from her eyes, soaking her pillow, she finally gave up trying to go back to sleep and pushed herself up into a sitting position. She brought her legs up and wrapped her arms around them, resting her forehead on her knees. She ignored Major, who padded over to the bed and whined.

"Father God," she whispered, her voice raw, "please help me. I don't know how much longer I can do this."

Knowing her own words wouldn't suffice, she reached over and took her Bible off the nightstand and flicked on the lamp. She opened the Word to Psalm 35. The picture of Esther fell out. Righteous anger welled up in her heart and overrode the fear. As a defense against the pain, the horror, and the hatred, she began reading out loud. "Let them be confounded and put to shame that seek after my soul: let them be turned back and brought to confusion that devise my hurt. Let them be as chaff before the wind: and let the angel of the Lord chase them. Let their way be dark and slippery: and let the angel of the Lord persecute them." She read the words over and over again until her heart settled, and peace returned. "And my soul shall be joyful in the Lord: it shall rejoice in His salvation."

Thirsty, she pushed out of bed and saw that she'd managed to sleep until four this morning. Nearly a record. With Major at her heels, she left the bedroom and went into the kitchen. She'd loaded the coffee maker the night before, so it only took hitting the button to start the brewing process.

While her coffee brewed, she opened the cupboard above the refrigerator and took down a whiteboard with rubber tubing stretched across it and a length of suture. Securing the board to the counter with the suction cups on the base of it, she practiced a one-handed surgical knot, intent on keeping the muscles in her hands strong and her muscle memory intact.

As the terror from her dream faded, anger made her

hand tremble, and she messed the knot up. Frustrated, she tossed the suture down. She held shaking hands against her eyes, whispering a mantra of a prayer, begging God for continued strength and protection. Major sat up and perked his ears at her, cocking his head as if listening for a command.

She poured a cup of coffee and patted the top of her thigh. He jumped up and rushed to the back door. She always let him go out first, knowing he'd sound an alarm if anyone waited out there. When he ran around the yard once and ran back to her, tongue waving, his open mouth making it look like he had a big grin, she stepped outside with him and slid the door shut behind her.

The early morning darkness enveloped her. Never quiet, the Florida wildlife sang to her—crickets chirping, tree frogs grunting, and birds already greeting the morning with a song. She settled into a chair on her porch and watched as Major made his rounds. Without that dog, she would have completely lost her courage and likely gone insane long ago. He'd given her companionship, protection, and a sense of security like nothing she could have imagined.

When he finished exploring the yard, he trotted to her and sat next to her chair. She slowly ran her hand over his head and down his back, enjoying the feel of his silky fur under her fingers. Her fingers located the scar above his right front leg, left there by the brutal assault with a knife. He whined a bit and lay his head in her lap.

Eyes closed, she thought about the message she'd received yesterday, and about the court date coming up. She spent the next thirty minutes in prayer and meditation, drawing on the strength and peace promised and provided by God.

Victor sat on the park bench and watched the pigeons fight over the piece of Danish he'd tossed their way. He smiled at the comical scene as he took a sip of coffee and leaned his head back, looking at the blue summer sky through the leaves of the tree. At seven in the morning, the heat had already started to rise. When he'd walked out of his apartment that morning, he'd anticipated stepping into cool air, not the muggy closeness he'd encountered.

Instead of his usual neighborhood jog, he went to the gym so he could work out in the air conditioning. His old trainer, Joe, would call him a little girl for choosing comfort over a good run, but he just called it old. At thirty, he'd spent a couple years longer than he probably should have in the boxing ring. Now he felt old and lackadaisical long before his time.

His favorite Bible character was King David. Knowing the hard, physically demanding life he'd led, Victor often wondered if David felt this worn out at his age. Had coming rain made his joints scream in pain? Could he feel every micro-fissure in his hands as the cold nights settled into the city?

An assortment of championship light heavyweight belts and trophies hung on the wall in his apartment. For seven years, he had dominated the world boxing arena and had, in many cases, been a household name. Now his name meant something else, something much darker.

Hearing footsteps, he looked up, and his heart skipped a beat. He sat up straighter, then realized the German shepherd on the end of the leash coming toward him wasn't Major, and the young red-haired woman jogging by in her green spandex wasn't Ruth.

With a wave of bitterness, he downed his coffee and stood. What he wouldn't give to set the clock back six months and a day. The things he'd do differently—the decisions he'd make....

He wondered if Marco's program would find her. He shook his head. He couldn't dwell on that right now. With his father in prison, he had a business to run. With a sigh, he ambled out of the park and to his father's office above the gym on Fifth.

Bypassing the public door, knowing the gym would be full of boxers and martial arts fighters intent on performing their daily regimens, he went up the outside stairs to the second floor, turning the lights on as he walked through the doorway. In the outer entryway, white tile floors and scarred mint green walls greeted him. A couple metal chairs sat around a dented and bent plastic table. The harsh fluorescent light flickered a bit as the ballasts warmed up.

At the inner door, he entered a numeric code on the keypad and entered his father's sanctuary. Here, cream wallpaper accented with gold flourishes papered the walls, and Oriental rugs lay scattered over a gleaming teak wood floor. Large leather couches formed a seating area around a low glass and gold table, and a massive desk worthy of the don of the Kovalev Empire sat on the far side of the room flanked by statues of medieval

Russian knights, swords drawn and ready.

Despite the illegality of most of the Kovalev business dealings, Antoly had run his company like a Wall Street corporation. Managers and assistants kept meticulous records and receipts—in code—of all business dealings.

When Victor sat in the desk, sometimes he could convince himself that everything he worked on was actually legitimate. Rarely did the real world penetrate the sanctity of this office. He wondered if that's how his father managed to do what he did—the weapons, the women, the drugs—for so long, by shielding himself inside the meticulous code, by pretending it was truly art shipments or the stock market.

Focusing on the business at hand, he pulled the large desk chair out and settled in to work. An hour later, a burly guard with a brown leather shoulder holster over his black T-shirt brought him a cup of coffee and handed him an itinerary for the day. He noticed that he had a meeting with his father's attorneys after lunch. With a sigh, he looked at his watch.

They would coach him on what to say when on the stand, then teach him how to sound like he hadn't been coached. For the next week, meetings with attorneys would dominate his schedule, he knew. He had an afternoon appointment he would have to reschedule, so he began the complicated workflow of sending a message and changing the meeting to late that night.

Chapter 6

At noon, Mara closed the lid on her laptop and rolled her head on her shoulders. She slipped the earphones out of her ears and pushed away from the table where she'd spent the morning transcribing notes from a pediatrician's office. With her stomach growling, she filled Major's food bowl, then made herself a sandwich from the chicken salad she'd made the day before. As she added a handful of tortilla chips to her plate, she heard a knock at her door.

Major rushed the door and wagged his tail, stilling her suddenly racing heart. She opened the door to Ben, who lifted his hand in a greeting. "Get back, silly," she said to Major as Ben opened the screen door. "Give him room to come inside." She smiled at Ben. "Hello!"

"Would you like to get some lunch?" Ben asked, petting Major who had pushed up against him.

"I just made a sandwich. There's plenty. Come on in."

He followed her into the kitchen, and when she saw the suture practice board still on the counter, her stomach fell. She gathered it up and hoped he didn't see it, sticking it under the sink instead of in its regular place above the fridge. When she turned around, she could see the question on his face but ignored it. "I have chicken salad."

"That's great," he said, moving to the sink to wash his hands. "I appreciate it. I was actually going to treat you."

"I've been looking forward to this sandwich all day," she said, loading chicken salad on a bread slice. "My world-famous chicken salad recipe courtesy of my sister, Esther." She paused, realizing what she'd just said. How could she let her guard down?

"I thought you didn't have any family," Ben replied, taking the plate from her.

"I don't." She cleared her throat as she took a pitcher of tea out of the refrigerator. "She died right before I moved here."

She poured them each a glass, and they sat at the table. After a brief prayer thanking God for the food, she took a bite of her sandwich, nearly choking when Ben said, "Is that why you don't work in the medical field anymore?"

Her eyes flew to his face as she took a drink of tea to wash down the food in her mouth. "Why would you—?"

"I'm pretty observant, Mara. I watched you with Jeremy. I listened to how you spoke to the paramedics. You clearly were something. Nurse, doctor, paramedic, something."

Her mind raced through the years of schooling and the stethoscope she'd left hanging on the hook next to her white coat in the locker at her hospital. Deciding she valued Ben's friendship enough to give him something, she nodded and let the tears fill her eyes. "You're right. I was a third-year surgical resident when they found my sister's body. Or what was left of her body. I had to take a break. I had to get out of the city."

He clearly hadn't expected her to open up that way. With wide eyes, he reached over and took her hand. "I'm sorry I've been so hidden and closed off. This has been the hardest six months of my life. I can't think of before. I can only think of the future."

"What future do you want?"

"Freedom," she whispered, pulling her hand away and taking another sip of her drink. The ice rattled in the cup with the trembling of her hand. "I want a future that is free."

He raised an eyebrow. "Free from what?"

"Fear." Major came up to her and lay his head in her lap. He knew not to come to the table with food present, but because he clearly came to comfort her, she didn't correct him.

"Are you afraid that what happened to your sister will happen to you?"

She paused, her hand resting on Major's head, and looked him dead in the eye. "I know it will. Just a matter of time. The only question is, will I be able to finish what I started before it does?"

Ben frowned. "I don't understand."

She gave a small smile. "I know." She picked up a chip and waved it in his direction. "I can't tell you about it, though."

With a sigh, he said, "Mara, I want—"

"I know what you want, Ben. I do. I'm not oblivious," she sighed and put the chip down without biting it, "but I can't give it to you. I can't. It's not fair of me, I know, but I value your friendship and don't want to lose that."

He studied her for several minutes before nodding his head. "You won't." He picked up his sandwich and smiled. "World famous, huh?"

Knowing he intended to act like the entire conversation never happened, she silently thanked him and nodded. "You'll never be able to look another chicken salad in the eye. I promise."

Six Months Ago

Victor opened his eyes, startled, and immediately the throbbing in his head worsened. He'd taken a pretty good hit tonight in the practice ring and had experienced enough concussions in his lifetime to know the symptoms. Joe had sent him to rest on the couch, knowing that if a doctor saw him, he would likely pull him from the fight. The way he felt right now, he didn't think he could even fake feeling fine in two days. He wondered if his last match would have to be a forfeit due to head injury.

What had wakened him? Then the sound came again, the raised voice of a man, begging for his life. As he squinted in the dim light of Joe's office, he tried to figure out where the sound came from. Rolling into a sitting position on the couch, he groaned and put his head in his hand, trying to focus less on himself and more on the man's voice.

The gunshot startled him. It sounded like it came from right outside the window. Pushing himself to his feet, he stumbled forward and headed to the window. Halfway there, he heard another gunshot. By the time he made it to the window, he spotted Vyacheslav Markoff, one of his father's lieutenants, and three bodies on the ground at his father's feet. Gripping the windowsill with both hands, tears streaming out his eyes, nausea rolling in his stomach, he stared at the man who contributed to half of his DNA and felt hate like nothing he'd ever felt before well up inside his chest.

Suddenly, his father turned and looked in his direction. He stepped back away from the window, thinking he'd seen him, but no, he didn't look right at the window, just in the general direction. He said something to Vy, who turned and sprinted down the alley. His father stepped over the bodies and followed at a walk.

What had just happened?

He turned and leaned his back against the wall, sliding down until he crouched near the floor. He would go tonight. He'd pack his mother a bag, send her away, and go to the hospital to find Ruth. He must, at all costs, convince her to run away with him. The world knew this weekend would be his last fight, and he knew the moment he retired from boxing, his father would expect him to start learning the family business. He would not. He could not.

Scrubbing his face with his hands, he stood. He would sneak out before his father saw him. He'd never even have to know he was here tonight, would never know he witnessed anything. He stumbled into the doorway and put his head in his hand. He sought inner strength to keep walking. He had to get out of the building before Antoly and Vy returned. With a push, he stumbled into the hall and ran right into Vy's chest.

Victor had to crane his head to look Vy in the eye. The giant had tattoos running up his neck and behind his shaved head—images of his beloved Russia permanently marked all over his body. Clearly, Victor had startled him because his eyes bugged out, and he put a hand on his shoulder. "Where were you?" he demanded in Russian.

Victor gestured over his shoulder with his thumb. "Took a hard blow to the head. Joe had me resting." He made a show of looking around, knowing his father would have emptied the gym to conduct his business. "Where did everyone go?"

Antoly walked down the hallway. "We had a meeting." He stopped next to the two men and looked at his son, his eyes skimming him from the top of his head to the toes of his sock-clad feet. "How's the head?"

"I think I have a concussion. I was on my way to the hospital."

"If Joe wanted you to go to the hospital, he would have sent you." He put his hands on Victor's cheeks, framing his face with his hands. "You and I, we need to have a talk about your girlfriend." He lifted his hands and slapped them back down, hard. The pain in Victor's head bounced around like the ringing of a bell. His stomach turned. Fear, disgust, anger, the pain in his head, and now on his cheeks—Victor tried desperately to maintain control, to not give anything at all away to the evil man in front of him. He felt his hands form into fists but very consciously relaxed them. "A very serious talk, Victor."

"About what?" How could she have anything to do with what happened tonight? Terror seized his heart. The idea that his father thought Ruth had anything to do with his business—

Antoly let go of Victor's face and stepped back, drawing a gun out of his holster and putting the barrel against the center of Victor's forehead. He felt his blood freeze to ice, and his heart pause.

"She's a threat to my entire organization. I should kill you for bringing her here. After all, I can just make another son." His eyes burned with intensity. This was not the first time he'd struck terror in Victor's heart, but it certainly topped the charts. "*Nyet*. No. Instead, I will kill her, I think. And I will enjoy your suffering. You need to learn a lesson, too." As he lowered his Tokarev, he looked at Vy. "Where is Lev?"

"Here," Lev Genrich, the thick man with the helmet of black hair said, coming into the hall. "I could not catch the cab. I have no idea where they went."

"Father—"

Antoly rounded on him. "You shut your mouth! Do not speak again!" Spittle flew out with the words. Then, calmly, he turned back to Lev. "Go to her apartment. When she comes home, make sure she understands my message."

Horror at the order he'd just heard gnawed at his stomach. "What?!"

Antoly put the gun barrel to his forehead again. "I said, shut up." As Lev left the building, he let in the man Victor knew as Mr. Kester, the contractor who provided cleanup services for some of his father's more heinous crimes. He hid bodies, erased evidence, and provided alibis when needed. He wore a perfectly tailored black suit with shoes shined to a high gloss. "I'm glad you were available. The mess is in the alley." He holstered his gun again and added, "There was a witness. I'm sure the cops will be here soon. Make sure there's no trace."

A witness? Dear God, had Ruth been here tonight? He had to get to her. He started to step away when Vy caught his arm. Antoly rounded on him. "Victor. Help Mr. Kester."

He closed his eyes, praying for patience and protection. "I have a concussion. I need medical attention."

Antoly stepped forward, his toes hitting Victor's. "You will help Mr. Kester with the three bodies in the alley, or else there will be four bodies. Do not think I would even hesitate before killing you, son of a harlot. You are easily replaced."

Turning his father against him would solve nothing. His mother had taught him that from birth. He clenched his teeth together and gave a short nod. "I apologize for any disrespect. My head hurts, and it's affecting my judgment. Please forgive me."

Antoly scowled. "I will forgive you when you get this mess cleaned up." He turned to Vy. "Those idiots out there lost ten grand. See what you can do to recover it."

Victor followed Mr. Kester out into the alley and

swallowed against his stomach's reaction to the line of dead bodies.

Chapter 7

Present Day

Mara ran the sweeper under the pulpit. For some reason, in the sanctity of this building, even without Major next to her, she never felt afraid, never felt like looking over her shoulder. As the song on her MP3 player changed to the next one, she looked out over the pews and smiled. She had loved every minute of working on this building and would miss it when she left one day.

As she rewound the sweeper cord back in place, the side door opened, and Brenda rushed in. Mara frowned and slipped the earbuds out of her ears. "What's wrong? Is Jeremy okay?"

Brenda dashed up the steps to the podium. "Oh, Mara, thank God I found you." She held out yesterday's newspaper. "Jeremy told me that a reporter came and talked to him, but he didn't tell me that he'd given her pictures, too!"

Her stomach turned to water, and her pulse pounded

in her neck painfully. She stared at a picture of her face taken while she tied the tank top onto Jeremy's leg, right there on the front page of the lifestyle section of the Gainesville newspaper. How many thousands of people got that newspaper daily? How many online sources ran the headlines?

Brenda said something, but she couldn't hear her through the roaring in her ears. The safety she had felt moments earlier vanished as if it had never existed. "I have to go," she whispered, dropping the cord she clutched in her hand. Leaving her friend standing on the stage, she jumped down and ran down the aisle.

When she burst through the doors and into the hot Florida sunshine, she felt the world start spinning around her. "What to do, what to do, what to do?" she whispered over and over again. Seconds later, the phone in her hand vibrated, startling her so that she nearly dropped it. She recognized the number and answered, saying by way of a greeting, "Get me out of here."

"I'm on my way," Federal Marshal Dean Tucker replied. "Forty minutes."

"That's too long," she sobbed.

"Do you want me to send local law enforcement?"

"Yes, yes." Disconnecting the call, she rushed across the street. Bursting into her house, she ran to the bedroom, grabbing a bag from the closet floor. It contained her life. Her entire thirty-year life fit inside one leather satchel. She went into the kitchen and put two days' worth of dog food in a plastic bowl, sealed the lid, and added that with a couple bottles of water and an empty bowl to the bag.

When she looked at her phone, she saw that only five minutes had gone by. Major followed close at her feet as she went into the living room, whining as he clearly sensed her distress. "We're okay," she said to the dog, not even sounding convincing to her own ears. "We'll be okay."

At the knock on the door, Mara's heart stopped, but Major jumped up and ran to the door, wagging his tail frantically. Ben must have seen her run across the street, or Brenda found him and told him what she'd said about hiding from an ex. She opened the door, and Major burst past her, throwing the screen door open with his weight and launching himself at the man standing on her porch.

After meeting Major on the ground and petting him and hugging the dog to him, the man greeted her in an all too familiar voice, simply saying, "Hello, Ruth."

Her heart stopped beating. It must have. Had he already shot her dead?

Victor Kovalev rubbed Major's fur and looked up at her. He hadn't changed in six months. He still wore his black hair cut short to combat the natural curls. While his mouth smiled, his light brown eyes looked at her with a serious, almost cautious expression. She licked her dry lips and looked past him, expecting to see a car full of hitmen unloading onto her lawn.

Clearly, Major offered no protection against her enemy. Feeling betrayed, she stepped out onto the porch. She'd known this day would eventually come, hadn't she? "Major, down," she said sternly. Immediately, Major stopped dancing and jumping around Victor, and lowered himself to the ground, his entire body vibrating with excitement. Should she run? Should she wait for the police that Marshal Tucker called to arrive?

She couldn't outrun him. Instead, she would stay outside, surrounded by neighbors who would hear if she needed help—witnesses to her coming death. She clenched her fists so he wouldn't notice her hands shaking. "The police are already on the way. They should be here any second."

"Well then," he said in his rich baritone voice with a curt nod. "I guess I better get this over with quickly." He reached into his pocket, and she opened her mouth to scream.

Six Months Ago

Victor stood outside Ruth's apartment and watched the blue lights of the police cars light up the street and buildings all around with an alternating blue and white strobe that made his eyes hurt. His head seemed to beat in rhythm with the strobe. He kept his hands shoved in his coat pockets, and his collar turned up against the wet snow that had started falling an hour ago but felt none of the cold. Instead, rage burned inside his heart that warmed him from the inside out.

If any of the officers swarming around had looked carefully at him, they would have seen the dirty boots and muddy jeans. He hoped they didn't see or ask about them because his brain had ceased working altogether, and he could not come up with an answer other than, "I spent the last three hours burying the bodies of the men my father ordered killed."

He had no doubt what such a large contingent of city vehicles meant. An hour ago, the coroner had arrived. He knew better than to hope that this was anything other than his father's handiwork. Stomach churning, head aching, eyes burning, he watched as the body was carefully brought down the steps and loaded into the back of the van.

When he saw an officer carry the body of faithful Major out of the building, he turned. Tears sliding down his face, he walked away, feeling more purposeful and determined with every step he took. As he walked, he looked up an address on his phone. As soon as he had it memorized, he turned the phone off and removed the battery. No one needed to know where he was going.

Fury fueled his steps as he turned onto Federal Plaza and walked to the glass doors of the Federal building. Without hesitation, he crossed the wide expanse of the lobby and marched up to the man at the duty desk. "My name is Victor Kovalev. I'm here to speak to your Organized Crime division regarding my father, Antoly Kovalev, and his brother, Boris Kovalev."

The man behind the desk picked up a phone and dialed a three-digit extension. Within seconds, he said, "You need to get down here."

Chapter 8

Mara watched as Victor slowly withdrew his hand from his pocket. She had expected him to pull out a gun. Then she remembered the sight of her sister's mutilated body and bitterly thought maybe he preferred a knife over a gun.

Just as her throat formed a scream, however, what he held in his hand stopped any sound from coming out of her mouth. As he extended his hand toward her, she realized he held the engagement ring box.

She wouldn't fall for any trap. Her voice came out angry, harsh. "I don't want it."

Sadness filled his eyes. He slipped the box back into his pocket and looked over his shoulder. "Can we talk, Ruth?"

"No." Little dots danced in front of her eyes, and her stomach turned as she thought of Esther's remains that she'd been forced to identify.

"I have so much I need to tell you, but—I don't think—"

"Is there a problem, Mara?" Ben asked, walking up her path. Major's ears perked up, and he vibrated with excitement, but he didn't move.

Victor's smile did not reach his eyes. "Mara, now, is it? Very clever." In the Bible, Ruth's mother-in-law, Naomi, had changed her name to Mara after her husband and sons died, because Mara meant bitterness. Ruth felt the name fit her circumstances and the state of her heart just fine.

Feeling like her face would crack if she tried to smile, she simply shook her head. "No, Ben, thank you." Her mouth was so dry that the words coming out sounding so normal surprised her. "He's looking for someone who isn't here."

Victor stared at her for several seconds before nodding and stepping off the porch. "It was good to see you again. I hope I'll see you next week. Think you'll make it?"

"With every ounce of strength I possess," she snapped.

He turned, stared at Ben as if sizing the man up, then walked away without a backward glance. As he walked away, she lowered herself onto the chair on shaking legs. She patted her thigh, and Major moved to sit next to her chair, putting his head in her lap.

"Who was that?" Ben asked.

"Someone from another life." She gestured at the chair next to her.

He did not sit. Instead, he stood in front of her,

leaning back against the railing. "What life might that be?"

Panic caused her heart rate to stay up. Her eyes scanned the street. Where were the police? "I have to go away." A single tear slipped out of her eye.

Ben knelt in front of her chair and took her hand with both his. His skin felt burning hot compared to her icy fingers. "Go away, where? For how long?"

She licked her lips. "Ben." After pulling free, she pressed her hands to her chest over her heart, willing it to slow down before it burst completely out of her chest. "I'm sorry. I won't be back. Not ever."

With a frown, he said, "I don't understand."

"I'm a federal witness in a case against a Russian mafia boss." When his eyes widened, she gave a small smile, knowing how absurd it sounded, even to her own ears. "I witnessed a killing, a triple murder, actually. Execution. And when I went to the police, they came looking for me. While I sat in a police station giving my statement, they found my sister at home. Major did what he could to protect her, but they—" Her breath caught, and she found she couldn't verbalize the carnage. She reached forward and cupped his face with her hands. "I am so tired of lying to you. I want you to know that if anything had been different, if my circumstances—"

She looked up as a police cruiser pulled up to her curb. Desperate to leave, she surged to her feet, nearly knocking Ben over. When she rushed inside for her bag and Major's leash, Ben followed her. "Stay," he pleaded.

"I can't!" she closed her eyes, tears falling down her face, and put a hand on her forehead. Think, she told herself. What was she missing? Had she forgotten anything? When she opened her eyes again, Ben stood almost toe-to-toe with her.

"Then let me go with you." Putting his hands on her shoulders, he gave them a small squeeze. "Mara—"

Taking a deep, deep breath, then slowly letting it out, she started to feel calmer. "I can't, Ben. You are an amazing man of God, but I am not the one for you. I can't let you risk your life for me. I won't." She leaned forward and kissed his cheek. "Thank you. You have no idea how much you have helped me."

When she pulled away, he did not follow her, nor did he insist on going with her. He stood in her doorway and watched as she snapped the leash on Major's collar and walked down the path to the cruiser.

Six Months Ago

Victor sat at the table and stared at Special Agent Rick Luther, who looked utterly starched and pressed even at three in the morning. "You're telling us that you had nothing to do, at all, with the operations of the Kovalev Empire?"

His neck prickled with annoyance at the question. So far, the agent had asked that same question three different ways. "I did not. I am a professional boxer. My father agreed to let me focus exclusively on boxing until my retirement, at which time the understanding was that I would start learning the family business. What don't you understand?"

"I understand what you're saying, Mr. Kovalev. The

problem I'm having with it is that you don't have anything for us."

He narrowed his eyes at the agent. "What do you mean?"

"I mean, you coming in here, ready to throw your father to us, means nothing." He laced his fingers on top of his father's file. "You have no testimony to give me that would convict your father. Which means, to use the common vernacular, you got nothing."

Victor sat back in his chair and ran his hands over his face. His eyes burned with fatigue. "What do you need?"

"Your father is too cautious. There's a reason we haven't put him behind bars yet." He looked up as the door opened. "I don't think you can give me anything I need. From what you've told me about the events of last night, I feel confident in believing that he won't trust you." He stood when the agent at the door beckoned him. "Excuse me."

Victor inhaled deeply and slowly let his breath out. All of this, for nothing? What good did it do to be Antoly Kovalev's only son? Not even the FBI appeared impressed with that. He closed his eyes and sought out a moment of peace with God. Despite the helpless feeling by which he currently felt swamped, he knew God would guide his next steps, whatever those may be.

"We might just have caught a break," Agent Luther said, taking the chair next to Victor rather than across from him. "Your father has been arrested."

"Arrested?" Confusion rippled through his tired mind. "What do you mean?"

"Your girlfriend showed up at an NYPD station

outside of your father's territory. The body you saw belonged to her sister, Doctor Esther Burnette. Not Ruth."

Overwhelmed, he rested his forehead on the table and miserably failed to hold back a sudden sadness. Silent tears streamed out of both eyes and puddled on the table. Relief over Ruth's survival warred with mourning over losing Esther. Fresh anger surged through his heart. If only he had a way to make all of this stop.

Special Agent Luther interrupted his internal battle for control. "Here's your chance," he said as if he'd heard Victor's thoughts, "to get in and infiltrate."

Victor shook his head as he raised it. With annoyed swipes of his scarred boxer fists, he wiped his cheeks dry. "No way. Boris would never trust me. The woman I brought into the fold—"

"Boris Kovalev is the dumb muscle. I think even he knows it. Humble yourself. Play the doting son and nephew. He'll likely be relieved if you step up."

As he thought about his father's empire, his lip curled in disgust. "Do you understand what they do? The drugs, the women?"

"Listen—"

The sound of his hand slapping the wooden table sounded like a gunshot in the room. "No! You listen. Every minute I sit in here, thousands of women are being held and used against their will. Thousands all over the world." He leaned forward and tapped his finger on the statement he'd made to that effect. "Every minute. If I do what you want, I'll have to—" The thought made him swallow. Concussed, exhausted, having ridden an emotional rollercoaster for the last few hours, he felt dizzy and nauseated. "I can't do it to them."

Agent Luther sat back in his seat and scrubbed at his face with his hands. "What you've given us isn't enough to stop it." He crossed his arms over his chest. "It simply is not. It's all guessing and hearsay. If we want to make a conviction stick against anyone other than your father, then you're going to have to give us more. Solid, firm, unshakable proof."

He'd given them all he had. Closing his eyes with a sigh, he struggled with the knowledge that what this man in his perfectly starched white shirt and pristine blue silk tie said was absolutely the truth. If he wanted to put a stop to it forever, he'd have to give them real evidence. "I'll have to commit crimes in order to maintain a good cover. If I am in any way wishy-washy, Boris will shut me out, and you'll get nothing."

Luther reached his hand over his shoulder, and a junior officer put a file folder in it. "I have immunity for you right here. We'll assign you a handler. Meet him weekly and give him physical evidence. Tell him everything you did, plan to do, and plan to order to have done. By the time your father's trial comes along, hopefully, we can arrest the whole lot of them."

He took the folder and opened it. In front of him lay a signed and sealed immunity deal. He could get into the organization. Boris would hand it over. He had no reason not to. He might bluster, but he would actually be relieved to not have to handle the details of the organization. Plus, he hadn't been there tonight. He didn't see how Antoly had spoken to him or what he'd said. Maybe he wouldn't get a chance to find out any time soon.

Knowing with certainty that this was absolutely the right decision, he picked up the pen and signed his name. As he put the cap back on the pen, he asked, "What next?"

Chapter 9

Present Day

Victor taxied down the runway of the little airport just outside of Philadelphia in his Piper Seminole. The little aircraft had made the flight back from Gainesville in just half a day. If everything went according to his carefully constructed plan, no one would ever know he'd even left the area.

Flying lessons had provided a release from the constant demands of training in the boxing ring. His daily regimen consisting of hours of working out, sparring, running, working out some more, then sparring again had completely taxed his body. Learning to fly gave him a way to exercise his mind and fine-tune his motor skills. When he'd won his first national championship, he'd bought the plane and stored it in a hangar on an airfield well away from the city. His father never once asked him what he did with the purse from the fight, and he had never volunteered the information.

After storing his plane in the hangar, he drove from the airport. He thought about Ruth and the absolute terror on her face when she'd seen him.

He could only thank God that he'd found himself sitting at the desk next to Marco's laptop when it sounded an alert. Ruth's face had shown up on a social media story. He'd deleted the alert and sent Marco to Maryland to meet with some outside contractors who were currently maintaining one of their online casinos. That bought him a good portion of the next two days to fly down to Florida to talk to the kid in the hospital.

It had taken no more than to pretend to be a member of the press following up on such a fantastic story of how she saved this young man's life. Within five minutes, he had Ruth's new name and address. Hopefully, his showing up on her doorstep made her scared enough to leave before Marco got back from Maryland and saw a thousand other alerts from that snakebite story and dispatched a Kovalev team to handle her.

As he headed into the Lincoln Tunnel, he worked out the full cover story for his absence. He pulled into the parking lot of a little family hotel and exited his car into the blazing summer heatwave that currently pummeled the city. Absently, he hit the lock button on his key fob as he entered the hotel, ignoring the bored desk clerk. When he got to his room on the fourth floor, he tapped on the door with the prearranged signal. In seconds, the door opened to a striking woman with ice-blue eyes and a mane of brunette hair wearing a denim mini-skirt and a black halter top.

"Hi, Mr. Kovalev," she greeted. Her tongue slowly

stroked her upper lip as she gave him a provocative stare.

As he walked in, he could smell the tang of garlic and tomatoes from the open pizza box on the dinette's counter. "How was your day, Nina?" he asked, pulling a wad of hundred dollar bills out of his pocket.

She pouted her lip but took the offered money. "It would have been nice to go outside."

He knew she preferred to sit in the hotel with pizza and free access to the remote control rather than working for his uncle, but he also knew she knew how to play an angle. "I agree." He looked at his watch. "After spending last night and the whole day together, we should go to a club. Why don't we go get you a dress and some new shoes, and we'll hit that new one on Eighth?"

Nina clapped her hands like a little girl. "Oh, Mr. Kovalev, yes! That would be perfect."

"And if someone asks where we've been all day?" Nina had provided him with an alibi a few times in the past. He knew he could rely on her.

She pressed toward him but did not touch him. "I'll ask them if they want details." She ran her tongue over her teeth before she stepped back and laughed. "I know exactly the dress I want. You're buying it, no?"

He gestured toward the door. "Of course. After you."

Ruth Burnette shed the Mara Harrison identity completely as she climbed into Marshal Dean Tucker's extended cab truck. The Marshal scratched Major's ears before letting him jump into the back seat. Ruth secured her seatbelt and watched as they rolled away from her little Florida home.

"This was a good place to be," she said quietly, feeling a pang of regret at the life she would never have a chance to live.

"Until you made the news." Dean looked at her in the rearview mirror. "I thought my boss would have an aneurysm when he saw your picture. What were you thinking?"

Thinking back to Jeremy, she gave half a smile. "That a boy would have died if I didn't act." She lay her head back and closed her eyes. No matter what, she knew she'd done the right thing. "I never thought about social media, or I would have put a stop to it before it started."

"Social media has made my job a little more complex than it was fifteen years ago." He plugged some coordinates into his GPS. "If the newspaper article hadn't happened, you could have come back here after the trial."

Keeping her eyes closed, she unconsciously shook her head. "No. It was time to leave." When she opened her eyes, she saw him looking at her. "The next place, I'd like to continue my surgical residency."

He nodded. "Getting back to work will be really good for you. I'll see what we can do."

"How can you do that? I won't have to start medical school over again, will I?"

He smiled as he shook his head. "No. We'll get you a transcript from a medical school. Everything will be arranged for you."

It stunned her just how smoothly the placement of WITSEC relocations appeared to happen. At least, it had been smooth for her. If she hadn't had to act to avoid the possible tragic death of a teenager, she wouldn't have had to disrupt the process at all, but the fact remained that he would have died if she hadn't acted. The only thing she'd go back and change if she couldn't change the presence of the snake in the first place was the ignorance that someone might post the story on social media. She wouldn't make that mistake again.

They drove to the Gainesville airport, stopping at a pet supply store to get a travel cage for Major. She administered the shot to give him a sedative and then led him into the cage. "There you go, boy," she said, feeling her eyes well with tears for her love for this animal who had protected her so fiercely for six months. "It will all be over soon."

Clearly already sleepy, Major whined and thumped his tail a few times before settling down and closing his eyes.

"All set?" Dean asked.

"All set." They walked side-by-side to the security gate. Dean took them over to the TSA Pre-check line and showed his badge and his authorization to carry his weapon beyond security. While Dean sidestepped the metal detector, Ruth put her backpack on the conveyor belt and walked through the security screening. Dean met her on the other side, and they walked to the gate.

Two men and a woman met them there. Dean Tucker knew the tall, dark-skinned man. "Marshal Andrew Brown, this is Ruth Burnette." They made introductions all around, and Dean handed Andrew a file folder.

He shook Ruth's hand. "I will see you after the trial when it's time to place you somewhere new. Andrew and his team will be your detail while you're in New York."

As he walked away, she couldn't help but feel a little panicked and abandoned. Instead of chasing after him, she turned to Marshal Brown and smiled, watching the other two Marshals as they casually took up positions that allowed them to watch everyone coming and going around the gate.

Marshal Brown looked at his watch as they sat in the uncomfortable plastic chairs. "We'll board early. Do you want a bottle of water or something?"

Worried about Major, worried about the trial, and worried about Victor Kovalev showing up on her doorstep, she pressed her lips tightly together and shook her head. Twenty minutes later, as she fastened her seatbelt, she leaned toward the marshal. "Will it be safe to be in the city so long before the trial?"

"We arranged a safe hotel for you," Marshal Brown said quietly, shifting to look out the window as the plane taxied. "Court starts Monday. I think we'll be okay for a long weekend."

She had four days to wait. At least at home, she'd have had the work at the church to keep her occupied. What would she do with her time? As she contemplated it, she determined that the next four days would be best spent fasting and in prayer.

Four days, then she'd start a new life all over again somewhere else. She'd really enjoyed the friends she'd made as Mara Harrison. Somehow, she didn't think she'd find another community like that one, but she knew with certainty that wherever she went, God had a plan for her.

Chapter 10

Ruth stood next to the window and looked down at Fifth Avenue, watching the heat rolling off the pavement in waves. The television newscaster said the heat index would reach almost one-hundred ten degrees today. It was much too hot to spend any time on the street surface. However, standing in an overly-air-conditioned hotel room, trapped inside, she longed to be down there on that burning hot street. She couldn't even take Major outside. A Federal Marshal came three times a day to walk him for her.

She'd spent the last three days fasting and praying. Despite what happened to her sister, she knew she had made the right decision and remained determined to testify. However, now that she had come to the moment, now that she was back in the city of her birth among friends she could never call, she deeply mourned the loss of her life.

She contemplated the dynamics of Victor's family. She thought back to the one time she'd had dinner with his parents. His mother, Zhanna, a strikingly beautiful blonde woman who looked young enough to be Victor's sister, didn't speak a lot of English but doted on Ruth. She cooked for them and hovered around them, continually touching Victor's hair or his shoulder.

Antoly, the father, came home minutes before the meal was served. He was cooler toward Ruth than his wife, but still somewhat welcoming. She watched the family interact, curious about how Zhanna and Victor did not seek Antoly out to engage him, yet pleasantly conversed with him when he initiated the conversation. She wondered about that because he seemed like a nice man.

After that evening, another four months went by before she even saw his parents again. In hindsight, she could see that Victor shielded her from his real life.

She curled her lip in anger and self-loathing. If only she'd thought to warn Esther before she went to the police station. Esther had died because of her, because of her bringing the son of a Russian mafia boss into their lives. The guilt weighed her down. She just wished she'd had some information that would help incriminate Victor as well.

A tapping at the door startled her. She checked her watch. The agent coming to walk Major was a full twenty minutes early.

Marshal Brown palmed his sidearm and looked through the door's peephole. He looked back at her, eyes wide, and motioned for her to get down while he drew his gun. Heart thumping, she knelt on the ground, and Major placed himself between her and the door, pushing up against her as if shielding her with his body.

Brown grabbed his ringing phone. Andrew looked at her as he spoke on the phone. "Yes, sir... Yes, sir... Understood." He straightened and lowered but did not re-holster his weapon. He opened the door, and a woman with teased brown hair wearing a silver bodysuit that stopped high on her thigh stepped into the hotel room.

"The Kovalevs know where you are," she said in a heavy Russian accent. Using her finger, she drew an oval in the air in front of her face. "Facial recognition software. I can help you get around the cameras. You have about five minutes before they're here."

Marshal Brown gestured with his head and held the door wide. "Let's go."

"How do we know we can trust her?" she demanded as she took a step backward, bumping into the window sill.

The young woman, who couldn't have been older than eighteen, put a hand on her hip. "They wouldn't send me to warn you. They'd have just shown up. You can trust me or not. I'm out of here. No way will I be caught with you when they get here."

Marshal Brown rushed toward her. "Let's go. I have orders to trust her." He held up his gun. "Cautiously."

After clipping Major's leash to his collar, she followed them out. In the hall, the woman said, "Keep your heads down. Step where I step and do what I do."

She ducked her head and sprinted toward the stairwell at the end of the hall. They took the stairs two at a time until they reached the ground level. With her hand on the exit door, the girl said, "Do not look to your left. Keep your head and face pointed to the right and hug to the building."

Sandwiched between the girl and the Marshal, she brushed against the building as they rushed down the alley. Thirty seconds later, they ducked into an alcove.

If Major hadn't lunged forward and if Marshal Brown hadn't been so close behind her, she would have turned and fled when she saw Victor inside the alcove. "Thanks, Nina," he said, handing her a folded bill. Fear gripped her, paralyzed her.

"Anything for you, Mr. Kovalev," she said, winking and taking the money. Without even looking at Ruth, she ducked out of the alcove and ran down the alley.

Victor looked at her and held both hands up. "I'm here as a friend. My cousin Marco, the family's hacker, got into the TSA system and found Ruth in the JFK terminal through facial recognition. For the last couple of days, he's been hacking the city's camera system, and they tracked her to this hotel."

Marshal Brown looked at Ruth, then Victor. "My people can't get here in time."

"You aren't going to trust him, are you?" Ruth demanded, finding her voice. "He killed my sister. His father is who I'm testifying against."

"He's good, according to my supervisor." He put a large hand on her shoulder. "No one wants to risk your life."

Victor shook his head. "Please, Ruth. You can fight with me later, but right now, you have to listen to me. I know the path around the cameras." He held out two baseball caps and sunglasses. "Put these on. And stick close to me."

Andrew checked the street, then Victor gestured, and they ran across the street and into the doorway of a boutique.

"No pets!" the salesclerk barked.

"Service animal," Ruth replied. She followed the men through the store, through the back storeroom, and out into the alley behind the building.

Victor and Andrew looked up and down the alley. The kitchen door of an Indian restaurant across the alley sat propped open with a box, so they crossed over and dashed into the kitchen. They raced through, amid the protests of the staff, through the dining room, and out onto the street.

A couple blocks sat between them and the hotel. Ruth put her hands on her hips and looked at Victor. Sweat poured down the side of her face. "What now?"

"We should go to the closest police station," Andrew said, looking at his phone.

"We're in Kovalev territory now, Marshal," Victor replied. "Ninety-nine percent of the cops are perfectly upstanding citizens. Unfortunately, it just takes one phone call." He put a hand on Major's head. "Stay with me. I'll get you somewhere safe until you can make other arrangements."

Victor looked around the corner of his building and spotted the girl in the short denim shorts and cropped tank top. She stood with her hand on one hip and casually blew a pink bubble with her gum. He knew she was fifteen, but her handler had put makeup on her to make her look a few years older. He gave a short whistle. Without turning to look at him, she casually waved at a passing cab, their signal that she hadn't noticed any of Boris' men nearby.

"All clear," he said, crouching down near Andrew, who peered around the corner of the building. "Go into that building, and immediately on the left, there's a stairwell. Third floor. Apartment 3-C."

Marshal Brown nodded and looked at Ruth. "Ready?"

She had barely looked at Victor unless she absolutely had to. Keeping one shoulder turned away from him, she nodded.

"Let the Marshal take Major," Victor said, reaching out and grabbing Major's leash, "then wait until he goes into the building and follow him."

When she turned to look at him, the vehemence in her eyes gave him pause. She did not answer him, simply jerked the leash from his hands, and held it out to the Marshal. Knowing she would soon know what he'd done, he let it go. She'd had no outlet for her pain for six months. It would seem that, for now, he would receive the full brunt of it. He had broad shoulders. He could take it.

As the marshal straightened and walked around the corner of the building to cross the street, Victor said to Ruth, "I'll see you in a few minutes."

"Where do you think you're going?" she spat.

"I have some work to do," he replied almost absently, watching the door shut behind Andrew. He tapped the brick wall with his hand. "Go. Don't look around. Just walk natural." As Ruth walked toward his apartment, he couldn't help but admire her strength. It took everything inside him to keep from pulling her to him and wrapping his arms around her, from promising her safety and security for the rest of her life. Obviously, he couldn't provide that. Everything he did from here on out would only protect her long enough until she could get away from him for good.

As soon as he heard the metal clang of the door shutting behind her, he straightened and walked into the street. He walked up to the girl who had given him the signal and slipped a hundred-dollar bill into the back pocket of her shorts. She never even glanced his way. He walked three blocks in the blistering heat to his uncle's gym.

By the time he went through the doors into the air conditioning, sweat had soaked through his shirt. Making a detour to the locker room, he whipped it off his head and changed into a fresh shirt. Twenty minutes later, he finished his third phone call and downed a protein shake as Marco came into the office and slammed the door shut.

"Someone tipped them off," he said in Russian. "The city, too. Their firewall just got a thousand times harder to crack." He narrowed his eyes at his cousin. "Where have you been for the last hour?"

Victor gestured at the whiteboard on the wall. "I've been arranging fights. We still have to operate a legitimate business, I have no idea where your father is, and with father's trial this week, there doesn't seem to be anyone else to do it. I'm doing my father's job and your father's job, too, it would seem."

"I don't believe you."

"No?" Victor threw the whiteboard marker at him like a dart, nailing him in the forehead. "Then, you do it. See if it's as easy and mindless as you imply."

Before he could react, Marco had him by the shirt front and pinned him up against the board. His eyes flared, a tell of a coming punch, and Victor waited until the last second to duck.

Marco's fist crashed into the whiteboard, cracking a dent in it right behind the spot Victor's face had occupied just a second before. Spinning, he grabbed his cousin's arm and jerked it high up on his back, pinning his face to the board. "You can't fight me and win, Marco. We both know that. I don't care how smart you are. You're physically weaker than me and always have been. You need me to break this arm for you?"

Marco fought against Victor's hold but couldn't break free. Finally, Victor pushed away. "I'm going to get some lunch. Stay out of my way."

He left the gym having sufficiently established his alibi. Worried, wanting to make sure Ruth was okay, he rushed back to his apartment. His lookout gave him a good signal, so he went into the doors and bounded up the stairwell. He heard Ruth's murmured voice giving Major a command as he put his key into the lock.

"Why are we here?" Ruth demanded, spinning in a circle in the middle of the living room. She imagined Daniel must have felt like this when he entered the lions' den.

Only, this den, this apartment, belonged to the man in front of her.

"No one will think to look for you here," Victor said, slipping into the apartment. He looked like he'd just run miles through a sauna. "I tipped off the city's IT department about the hacking, so for now, Marco is locked out, and I doubt he'll be able to get back in before tomorrow's trial."

Marshal Brown disconnected his call and slipped his phone into his pocket. "We'll have another location within the hour. For now, just relax."

"This is like a bad dream," she muttered, perching on the edge of the couch. "It's like you don't even realize who this man is."

Victor shook his head. "I was never that. Never. My mother made my father promise to keep me out of the family business. The closest thing I got to it was boxing, but I never even threw a match."

Ruth stared at him, her hands cold, her heart rate still a little higher than she liked. "I don't believe you."

He stood by the door. She could see the hurt in his eyes, but she didn't trust it. "I can't control that. That is your choice. Hopefully, by the time the trial is over, you will."

"Isn't that the whole point of the business?" she asked, nearly spitting out the word. "The family connection? Loyalty?"

He shrugged almost nonchalantly. "Possibly. Maybe there was a time when family loyalty might have swayed me." He walked toward her, and she resisted the urge to get up and move away from him. "When I met you, you introduced me to Christ. Accepting Him into my life knowing how much He loves me and sacrificed for me... I couldn't betray Him by having anything to do with my father's business dealings."

Her jaw clenched so tightly her back teeth ached. She purposefully loosened her muscles. "You were supposed to be there that night. At that gym where those men were killed. It happened where you worked, where you did your business."

Nodding, Victor said, "I was there. I was in Joe's office. I took a bad punch and was out of sorts. He sent me in there to rest and see if I needed to go to the hospital. I never knew—"

Marshal Brown's phone chirped. Ruth watched as he nodded. "Got it." He disconnected the call and stood. "We have a place." Looking at Victor, he said, "Good luck this week. What you're going to do won't be easy, despite all of the circumstances."

"Thank you. I appreciate that." He looked at Ruth. "I'll see you tomorrow."

Ignoring him, she gave Major a hand command, and they followed the marshal out of the apartment. Two blocks away, a dark Suburban waited for them. She climbed into the back seat and pulled her legs up to her chest, wrapping her arms around them. Closing her eyes, she prayed for strength for the next few days.

Chapter 11

Ruth took the witness stand and stared at Antoly Kovalev. He sat at the table in the front of the courtroom next to two of his attorneys. Behind their table sat an entire team of lawyers and legal aids. While she stared at him, he raised his fingers and pantomimed shooting a gun at her. Her heart skipped a beat, but she refused to give him any reaction other than raising one eyebrow and looking back to the lawyer who currently cross-examined her.

"So, you're saying, Miss Burnette—"

"Doctor," Ruth corrected.

The man with the Ken-doll haircut and gleaming teeth paused. "I beg your pardon?"

"I'm not a Miss. I'm a doctor. You can refer to me as Doctor Burnette, or you can find another lawyer to question me."

A murmur ran through the courtroom. Ruth felt like she'd gained a tiny bit of the upper hand in this battle of wills she'd fought for the last twenty minutes with this attorney. The man turned to the judge. "Your Honor—"

He glared at the lawyer over his half-moon glasses. "Yes, Mr. Mitchell?"

"Can you please compel the witness?"

The unsympathetic judge smiled, and in a sugar sweet voice said, "What shall I compel her to do, Mr. Mitchell? Her request is simple and understandable. Please address her correctly or find someone on your vast legal team who knows how to pronounce the word 'Doctor'."

A bit of color flooded the top of his cheeks, but he didn't reply. Instead, he turned back to Ruth. "So what you're saying, *Doctor* Burnette, is that you didn't actually see the defendant, Mr. Antoly Kovalev, here, with a gun in his hand?"

Images flashed in front of her eyes of Antoly Kovalev, smirking at the man on his knees, begging for his life. "I did not."

"So, in fact, you didn't witness him killing anyone?"

She almost visibly jumped when she re-heard the gunshot in her mind. "I did not."

"Isn't it true that Mr. Kovalev could have been there under duress as well?"

The prosecutor didn't stand. He simply said, in an almost bored voice, "Objection. Calls for speculation."

The judge answered, "Sustained. Mr. Mitchell, I'm getting tired of reminding you that you are not writing a fictional novel here. Quit setting up for your closing arguments and stick with just the facts."

Ruth had already testified to hearing one of the men begging Antoly Kovalev for his life. At this point, the attorneys just tried to get the jury to forget her testimony by dragging the cross-examination out for long minutes and making her admit to what she did not see over and over again. She had prepared for this, and did not rise to any bait, nor did she get defensive. She knew that any kind of hesitation or defensive posturing would possibly make the jury doubt the testimony she'd already given. In a monotone, she simply answered every question with absolute honesty, correcting them every time they dropped the Doctor from her name.

"Let's talk about your relationship with Victor Kovalev," the attorney said, his back to her, his eyes searching the jury box.

As if on their own accord, Ruth's eyes fell on Victor, who sat in the middle of the courtroom, watching her with a stoic expression. She missed him. No. That wasn't exactly right. She missed the relationship she'd had with the man she'd thought he was. She did not miss the mafia boss's son. She reminded herself that she also missed Esther.

Mr. Mitchell continued. "Isn't it true that you and Victor Kovalev had a lover's spat, and your testimony today is just your way of getting back at him?"

Curious where this man intended to take this, she simply said, "No."

"No?"

She raised an eyebrow. "Shall I spell it?"

A murmured giggle spread through the courtroom. Mr. Mitchell continued. "But you haven't been in contact with Victor since that night. Isn't that true?"

"I've spoken to him twice since that night."

He fumbled on his next words, then turned and looked at her with a confused look on his face. "Twice?"

"Yes."

He clearly didn't know that. It gave him pause. Recovering, he asked, "When did you speak with Victor Kovalev since that night?"

She knew the lawyer hadn't intended to open the door for her to talk about her sister's murder, but she thanked God for the opportunity anyway.

"Knowing the reputation of the Kovalev family and the danger my going to the police would place on my life, the Federal Marshals decided to put my sister into protective custody and in witness protection and me. When they went to my apartment to get my sister, they found her brutally murdered. Her tongue had been cut out of her mouth while she was still alive." A few gasps echoed around the room. "I knew, as the police knew, that I'd received a warning from Antoly Kovalev. Talk, and the same thing would happen to me."

"Objection!" one of the defense attorneys at the table interrupted.

Amused, the judge looked at Ruth. "You're objecting to the answer to your own lead council's question? Rather irregular, Ms. Bynes."

"Your Honor, this is not relevant. Mr. Kovalev has never been charged with the murder of this woman's sister. As far as I know, no one has been charged with that crime."

The bored sounding prosecuting attorney didn't even look up as he intoned, "Goes to state of mind."

"I tend to agree with the prosecution," the judge

said. "The witness is answering your question. Perhaps you should have been more careful about what you asked her." He looked at Ruth. "Please continue, Doctor Burnette."

"Thank you, sir," she said, then looked at Mr. Mitchell again. "I spent the next six months in witness protection. Last week, Victor found me."

"He found you?" Mr. Mitchell frowned, turning to look at Victor. He clearly didn't know whether to continue with this line of questioning.

"Yes. I had saved a teenager's life. He had been bitten twice by a very large rattlesnake. I'm afraid that pictures of my actions went viral on social media. The Marshals were on their way to relocate me when Victor showed up."

"I see." He opened his mouth, then shut it again and looked at Antoly Kovalev, who had turned in his seat to glare at his son. Finally, he looked at the judge. "Your Honor, may I have a few moments to confer with my client?"

The judge heaved an exaggerated sigh and looked at his watch. "If we must, let's go ahead and break for lunch. We'll reconvene at one o'clock." He hit the gavel, and the bailiff had everyone rise while the judge exited the courtroom through the back door.

Ruth waited for the Marshals guarding her to escort her through a side door and into a protected room. Seconds later, Victor entered the room, too. Ruth stood quickly and backed against the wall. "Why are you in here?"

"Because until someone returns with food for us,

they need us together. Manpower. There aren't enough guards for us that they trust."

That confused her. With a frown, she said, "I don't understand, Victor. Why are you under protection, too?"

"I wasn't going to be until after the trial. I'm sure right now my uncle is looking for me." As if on cue, his cell phone rang. He pulled it out of his pocket and turned it off. "As far as my family knows, when they put me on the stand, I will lie through my teeth and talk about the wonderful charitable acts my father performs on a regular basis. Instead, the plan is to kind of throw a proverbial curveball and just unload what I know about that night and all of my father's other illegal activities."

The muscles in her neck that had tensed up when he came into the room gradually relaxed. After the way he'd helped her yesterday, and now sat in the room under Marshal protection with her, a tiny amount of trust for him started to bloom inside her. "Why?"

"Why am I testifying against my family?" He reached into his pocket and pulled out the ring case, setting it on the table. Her heart twisted, reminding her of the depth of love she'd once had for this man, of the future she'd anticipated with all her soul.

"Because I love you, Ruth. Because the Holy Spirit is dwelling in me. My family, my father, and his kind, they're evil. What they do is wrong. I have enough information to put most of my family members behind bars for a very long time. I have information that will save a lot of women from living horrifying lives. I have locations of drug storage and weapons caches, of housing for the girls, and I am gladly sharing it." He looked at his watch. "I'm sure federal agents are raiding those places even now."

All the feelings she'd had for him that she thought had died along with Esther, all of them suddenly flooded her heart. As she realized his situation, she felt a rush of panic. She moved forward and sat in the chair next to him. "Victor, I'm no one special. Me, they're likely to forget. The threat against me will almost certainly dissolve when I walk out of this courtroom today or tomorrow. The damage will have been done, and they won't waste resources looking for me and taking on WITSEC."

Without thinking about it or talking herself out of it, she reached forward and took his hand. "But Victor, they won't ever stop looking for you. Do you realize that? What I've learned of this culture for the last six months tells me that the moment you open your mouth, you will perform an unforgivable act, and they will look under every rock until they find you."

He sandwiched her hands with his own. "My family have been criminals long before they ever came to America. I come from a long line of brutal killers and thieves—people who wear prison tattoos like badges of honor. If I can break the cycle, then I think that just might be worth my life."

His brown eyes bore intently into hers. "I know I won't ever be free again. That's why when we walk out of here, I'll go one way and you'll go another. But I wanted you to know that you are the one that brought about this change; that because of you, this city will be a better place for so many people. This is what I wanted to tell you when I went to Florida to see you. You and your love for God and your love for me is what has made all the difference in the world for countless innocent people."

He tapped the top of the ring box. "I'm thankful that we didn't get married. I believe God was protecting you from me when you felt compelled to tell me 'not now'."

She opened her mouth to protest just as someone rapped on the door, making her jump. The Marshal at the door took the bags of sandwiches from the one carrying the food in, freeing the other's hands to hand out the drinks. The moment she and Victor shared had passed. She circled back around the table and sat across from him.

After setting out the food, he reached across the table with his palm up. They'd held hands together and prayed over countless meals. The last piece of her hardened heart chipped away as she set her hand in his and closed her eyes. Familiarity washed over her as he prayed over their food. His hard, calloused hands felt so strong yet held her fingers so gently. His rich baritone voice washed over her as he quietly said a simple prayer of blessing.

As she bit into her turkey sandwich, she looked at him and worried about what he would need to do on the stand, and loved him more than she ever had before because of it. She quickly swallowed before she spoke.

"Tell me what happened? What went wrong that night?" She opened a bag of potato chips and sat quietly, waiting to hear his answer.

Victor picked up his cup and leaned back in his chair.

He took a long pull of soda through his straw before speaking. "I'd worked out, sparred with someone in the ring for a bit. Even with the helmet on, he hit me hard enough to daze me. Joe didn't like it. He didn't want me working anymore that night. I had that big fight coming up on New Year's Eve, and a padded hit nearly felled me. I went to Joe's office to lie down, see if the dizziness would pass without medical intervention."

The doctor in her raised an eyebrow. "Why not just go to the hospital?"

"Joe was worried a doctor would make me sit out the fight."

She pursed her lips. "For good cause, Victor."

He smiled despite their circumstances. "I won that fight. Did you know that?"

Biting her lip to keep from lecturing him, again, on the dangers of continued head trauma, she simply said, "I saw it in the paper." Taking a deep breath, she quickly spewed out the words. "How could you fight after what happened? Esther, your father—"

"I was told in no uncertain terms that I had to finish my career on a high and fight that fight." He picked up the paper cup and swirled the ice around in the remaining soda. "So, I fought. And I won."

Slowly, she wiped her fingers on her napkin, trying to decide how to word what she felt. "I don't understand how you lived with knowing who your father was," she paused, "I mean, it's not like you were twelve. You were thirty." Even now, that's what held her back from completely trusting him, and she knew it.

It took him several seconds to answer. For a while, he

looked at his half-eaten sandwich, then shifted his eyes to look intently at her. "My mother."

She immediately pictured the stunning woman who spoke very broken English. "Your mother?"

"My mother was taken from her home in Orenburg, Russia, when she was just fourteen years old. She's never been back. No reason to. Her parents, my grandparents, they both died just a few days after she left." A muscle ticked in Victor's cheek as he clenched his jaw. "My father—" he hesitated, let out a shaky breath, and then said, "My father was a wealthy businessman who funded many Soviet politicians. He bought her right after her fifteenth birthday. She told me once that she could endure being his wife because it was better than the manor where she'd worked for the woman who eventually sold her." He cleared his throat. "I was born in a mansion in Moscow just a few years before the collapse of the Soviet Union."

He took a bite of sandwich and chewed silently for a few moments. Washing it down with a sip of soda, he added, "It was easy for my father to shift to what he does now. He had been hoarding gold and diamonds for years. His moral compass had never worked properly. The switch from loyalty to the Kremlin to running weapons was as simple as changing his socks.

"Boris had served as an officer in the military. His weapons contacts were what tipped the scale for the Kovalevs to really dominate." As he sat back in his chair, he rubbed his knuckles, silently cluing her in to the fact that his hands ached. "And through all of it, he had this child bride he'd bought and stashed away, bringing her out when it suited him." He cleared his throat. "After my first championship, I begged her to come away with me, but she didn't want to leave him. Not for herself, but for fear that he would come after me."

The glimmer of hate in his eyes made her throat go dry. "He is very possessive of his possessions. After a couple of decades, she was so conditioned that she could shop, go to her stylists, go to spas, and act like a free woman. But her drivers were always armed men whose jobs were to contain her as much as protect her."

Six months ago, she wouldn't, no, couldn't have believed his story. A vague intellectual knowledge of such evil in the world never had penetrated her secure little bubble of Columbia University Medical School and the life around it. But in six months, she'd done a lot of research and knew that he spoke the absolute truth. "So, you stayed for her?"

Pushing away from the table, he surged to his feet and started pacing the confines of the little room. He loosened his tie and unbuttoned the top button of his shirt. Thinking back to the various times he'd complained about wearing a tie to dinner, or to a church function, warm memories flooded her mind. Despite the subject matter, a small smile formed on her lips.

"She somehow convinced my father that my boxing career was more important and that I needn't concern myself with the family business until I retired. For whatever reason, he agreed. I think he took a lot of personal pride in my accomplishments. The only possible reason he'd do anything for her was for his own benefit. I'd always planned on taking her away when I retired, somewhere away from him and safe, but then I met you, and I didn't know what to do, so I boxed for a few more years." Victor came to her side of the table and pulled out the chair next to her. She turned to face him, and he surprised her by taking both her hands in his. "I thought you'd been killed."

With wide eyes, she said, "Me?"

"I went to your apartment that night to warn you. The police were already there. I saw Esther—" Hot tears sprang to her eyes as a ravaged look of pain crossed over his face. "I thought it was you," he said in a gruff voice. "I couldn't bear it. I went to the FBI. When the guy on desk duty heard my name, I thought he was going to pass out." He bowed his head, pressing her knuckles into his forehead. "I told them everything I knew, and they said it wasn't enough. I had to go in, undercover, and learn more. Get solid evidence. For six months, I've done the one thing that my mother had prayed I wouldn't do—I ran the Kovalev mob."

Tears streaked down her face, and she leaned down, resting her cheek on top of his head, feeling the brush of his soft hair against her skin, inhaling the once familiar scent of his shampoo. What little she understood about the business, and how much she knew his heart, she couldn't believe he'd done that. "I can't imagine how hard that was."

"I just counted down the days to the trial. At least I had an end in sight." He straightened and peered into her eyes, their faces so close she could feel his breath against her cheek. "This morning, they put my mother in WITSEC. She would have gone sooner, but my mission was too important to risk discovery. For the first time in thirty-three years, she's free."

She put a shaking hand on his cheek. How hard would it have been for him to tell his mother goodbye? "And you?"

He closed his eyes with a sigh. "I will never be free." When he opened his eyes, the passion and intensity reflecting back at her took her breath away. "But you and my mother will be free. And that is what matters. That is all that matters to me."

Major kicked his legs and whimpered in his sleep. Reaching down, Ruth put her hand on his ribs, and he almost immediately settled down. She rested her head against the iron bars of the balcony and looked down at the quiet city street. At two in the morning, no one moved, and not even a car had rumbled down the street in twenty minutes. She tensed when she heard the glass door slide open, but when Major only opened one eye and lazily half-wagged his tail, she relaxed, knowing that Victor had come out on the patio with her.

She looked over at him and saw the guard on duty in the living room beyond the door.

"Couldn't sleep?" he asked, lowering himself down onto the concrete next to her.

"I have quite a bit on my mind," she said, almost absently. She looked back down at the street. Potted geraniums stood on either side of the steps like sentries in front of the Italian restaurant across the street. The street light made the coral color look like a deep purple.

"Do you miss the city?"

I miss you, she thought to herself, but she didn't say the words out loud. The things he'd told her in the courtroom just a few hours ago had changed so much of her perspective on things. The question that kept her awake right now was simply what she intended to do with that new perspective.

"I miss my life." When sorrow flooded her chest and her throat burned with tears, she angrily put her hand to her chest. No breaking down now. She'd promised herself when she got to her new home, she would spend a week allowing herself the freedom of breaking down whenever she felt like it. Right now, she still had to maintain calm. "I miss school, the hospital... Esther." Her sister's name came out in a whisper a second before the first sob overwhelmed her.

His arms came around her as naturally as breathing, pulling her tightly to his chest. It felt so good to be held by him again. She had missed him. Terribly. Even when she tried to convince herself that what she'd missed was her idea of him, she had missed him. Now, she sobbed against his chest as thoughts of the last six months overwhelmed her. She felt so angry at his father and his family for the things they had done to her and her family, to him. What would happen now? What would life look like when this trial ended?

At some point, the wracking sobs subsided, and she realized he held her in his lap, her cheek on his shoulder, his hands rubbing her back, his fingers running through her hair. An exhausted wave washed over her, and she closed her eyes, inhaling his familiar scent. It would be easy to press her lips against his neck.

Heat flooded her face at the direction of her thoughts, and she pushed away. "I'm sorry," she said, ducking her head. "I—"

Victor cupped her face with both his hands and raised her head, forcing her to look in his eyes. She could see the shine of unshed tears, the regret, and the emotions swirling in their coffee-colored depths. "Ruth," he whispered, seconds before his lips met hers.

Without a second's thought, she slipped her arms around his neck. As natural as breathing, she kissed him back, feeling her pulse hammer in her neck and her breath catch in the back of her throat. She tasted her own tears, felt his shuddering breath, inhaled the smell of him. Time faded away. Six months gone on a wisp of breeze, and she was back at the fast-food restaurant, kissing him goodbye for the last time.

Gradually, the kiss gentled until it was a mere brushing of lips and mingling of breath. Finally, she rested her cheek on his chest, keeping her arms around his neck. Twenty-four hours ago, she hoped she'd never see him again. Now, how would she ever tell him goodbye when this trial ended? For years, she planned on marrying him, building a life and a ministry with him. For months, she'd nursed a heart that had felt like someone had ripped it out of her chest. The emotional roller coaster threatened to overwhelm her, and she pushed away.

"We'd better get some sleep." Her voice sounded hoarse and strained to her own ears. Standing, she clicked her tongue to wake Major. "I missed you," she whispered.

He didn't speak as she let herself back into the apartment and walked to her room.

Chapter 12

Ruth learned that Boris Kovalev and one of his sons had disappeared. The police went to arrest them the day of her testimony and found a cleaned-out office and an empty apartment. In a single day, he shot up to the number one most wanted criminal in America. "Are you worried?" Ruth asked Victor over Chinese take-out.

He shrugged, grabbing a chunk of orange chicken with his chopsticks. "I'll just say that I'll be happy when the trial is over, and I'm no longer under armed guard." He gestured at the door. "The more people who have to protect us, the more people there are who know where we are. My family has a lot of pull and a lot of reach. We will be lucky to stay safe."

"Do you think they know what you'll say?"

He used his chopsticks to poke at his box of rice, but finally, just set it down. "I don't know. I don't know the level of their arrogance. My father certainly has no idea."

Ruth had a hard time falling asleep that night. Her mind swirled with memories, thoughts of how her testimony had gone, and worry over Victor's upcoming time on the witness stand. She listened to the murmur of voices coming from the Federal Marshals in the other room and Major breathing in his bed under the window.

Clinging to those sounds—those sounds that meant safety and some facet of security—she drifted off only to wake with a start just a few hours later. What had woken her up? Major still slept under the window but moved his paws and gave a little yelp in his sleep. She smiled, thinking of him dreaming his dog dreams, chasing a rabbit or maybe a deer.

Restless, she climbed out of bed. Major hopped up and followed her as she quietly left her room. She lifted a hand in greeting to the guard at the apartment door but did not stop to speak to him. Instead, she slid the glass door to the patio open and stepped out onto the concrete. Sheets of rain poured down, sending a cooling spray onto the porch. Major scooted back away from the wet, keeping his back to the door. Ruth laughed at him. "Don't want to get your paws wet?"

"He never did like the rain much, I remember."

Startled, she spun and saw Victor sitting in a chair angled away from the splash of rain. As her heart slowed back to a normal pace, she walked toward him and felt the seat of the chair next to his, checking to see how much rain had splashed on it, then deciding it was dry enough. "I hated rainy days in the city with him. In Florida, he didn't mind it too much. Probably because it rained so often."

"Maybe different smells associated with it. I remember Esther found him during a storm in the city.

Would have been terrifying for a little pup like he was." He held his hand out into the stream of water. "Do you think it will cool it down any?"

"Until the sun comes out and it all evaporates into steam. Then it will be like breathing underwater." She pulled her legs up and wrapped her arms around them. "Can't sleep?"

A wry look crossed his face. "Signing my own death warrant has taken a bit of a toll on my circadian rhythms."

"Victor—"

He shook his head. "I am doing the right thing. I went about it the right way, and there's a solid case now against everyone I know of in the family. I'll likely be testifying for months at different trials."

She studied his face in the faint light coming from a lamp inside the building, seeing a muscle tic in his jaw. "But?"

"But it's my father. And there's an emotional connection I didn't expect to feel. Something I'm severing with every word I will speak on that stand tomorrow. It was one thing to talk about it privately, in the office of the FBI. It will be another to look at him and say the words."

They sat in silence while Ruth digested what he said. Finally, she replied, "I can't pretend to understand that. But I know that to follow Christ, sometimes we have to leave the dead to be buried by someone else. I think that is fitting for your circumstance." She paused. "Have you ever tried to talk about God to your father?"

With a short bark of a laugh, he shook the water off his hand. "Once. He punched me in the jaw and told me to concentrate on winning my next fight and not some deity that had poisoned my mind. That was a couple of years ago."

Remembering the few times she'd had personal conversations with Antoly Kovalev, she said, "I imagine that trying was a bit intimidating."

Turning his head to look at her, his eyes reflected the weak lighting from inside the building. "There are so many things you couldn't possibly imagine, Ruth. The Kovalevs are evil, and I long for the day I sign the papers to change my name."

They sat on the porch until the rain stopped, and the sun started to rise. As the sky lit up with pink and yellow streaks, they both went inside and to their own rooms to prepare for the day. An hour later, she met Victor in the kitchen. He looked like he'd aged overnight. "I am praying for you today," she said with a forced smile, putting a coffee pod in the coffee maker and pressing a button.

"I know. I am drawing strength from that." He leaned against the counter. He wore a navy-blue suit with a white shirt and bright blue tie. "Hopefully, it will be over today."

"Then what?" she asked.

"Then we go into hiding. You go one way; I go the other."

She'd hoped that as they rekindled their feelings for each other over the last couple of days that his plan to leave her after the trial would have changed. "But—"

He shook his head as he straightened and dumped the remaining coffee in his cup into the sink. "But nothing. It's the only way you'll stay safe."

Feeling her heart break all over again, she tried to argue. "Victor—"

Without warning, he pulled her to him, wrapping his arms around her. She felt safe, shielded, secure. Closing her eyes, she rested her head on his chest and listened to the steady beat of his heart. His shirt smelled clean, but below that, she could smell the scent of him. Of Victor. Ruth took a slow, deep breath and drew his smell inside.

"I can't bear the thought of you being in danger anymore," he confessed in a gruff voice. "I cannot risk you. Please understand that."

Knowing how much he had sacrificed just to keep his mother safe, she knew he truly meant what he said. He didn't want to leave her for himself, he actually did feel like it would protect her. A tear slid out of her eye, and she did not speak. Instead, she hugged him tighter.

Twenty minutes later, they loaded into the back of a black SUV. Marshal Andrew Brown took the wheel. A female Marshal followed in an unmarked car.

"So, tell me about that pastor," Victor said with a teasing smile.

Ruth thought back to the little village in Florida. Her time there felt almost like a dream. "Ben? Good man. I enjoyed working with him."

"He was very protective of you," Victor observed. "He did not like the way you acted when I went there."

Thinking of that day—had it truly only been a week ago - she said, "He knew something was wrong with me, something in my life. He just didn't know what it was."

"He probably thought I was some abusive ex-husband who had hunted you down."

She laughed, a little uncomfortably, knowing that she intentionally guided that assumption. "No doubt." Almost immediately, her face grew serious again. "I hated deceiving him. The idea that I'll have to live a lie for the rest of my life is still a little unsettling." She ran her thumb over the fingers on her left hand. "I told them that wherever I go next, I want to be a doctor again."

"Again?" He smiled. "What were you before?"

She screwed her face up. "I did medical transcription. I tell you what, I learned what not to do when I record my—" Before she could finish her sentence, she found herself thrown against Victor, her seatbelt ripping into her chest and hips. The sound of metal grinding against metal screamed in her ears as the side of the SUV barreled into her.

Marshal Brown fought for control as the SUV slid through the intersection and crashed into an oncoming car. With the impact, her head hit the side window, dazing her. The next thing she knew, Victor had her face framed in his hands. She could see his mouth moving and could understand the intensity of what he said, but she couldn't hear anything through the ringing and roaring in her ears. The pain in her head made her vision jitter and jump. First, she saw two of him, then they merged into one as the ringing in her ears subsided, and his voice became clear.

"Now! Come on, Ruth, move!" Her stomach rolled, and she fought the impulse to lay her head back against the seat and close her eyes. She watched as Marshal Brown kicked the front windshield out and climbed out of it, pistol drawn. Victor reached over her and pushed the passenger door open. Ruth's hands slipped on the seatbelt twice before she managed to unbuckle it. Victor climbed over her and out of the vehicle, then crouched at the open door and held his hand out to her. "Come on!"

She felt like her brain disconnected from her body. As soon as she placed her hand in his, the panicked nausea that had started to overtake her withdrew along with the pain in her head. On her side of the vehicle, she could see the impression of the dump truck that had T-boned it. As she crawled, she glanced over the hood and saw two men get out of the dump truck, pistols in their hands. She heard the screams of onlookers before she heard the gunshots. The window next to her head suddenly cracked, shattering in a spider web pattern, and she heard the pings of bullets hitting the side of the SUV. A burning smell filled her nostrils, and smoke stung her eyes.

"Go!" yelled Marshal Brown as he crouched next to the tire. He held his phone up to his ear and looked at Victor. "Get to cover!"

She began moving on autopilot, refusing to let her mind process the sight and sounds of a gunfight in downtown New York. Without looking back, she held tight to Victor's hand as he led them away from the intersection. "Don't stop," he yelled, dodging his way through the heavy rush-hour pedestrian traffic. "We're in Kovalev territory." He shoved past a delivery man wheeling a cart full of boxes and looked over his shoulder at her. "Not safe."

He didn't say another word. As adrenaline pumped

through her system, her headache receded, and the pain she'd initially felt in her knee faded. Who knew what kind of damage she did to her body sprinting with an almost certain concussion and possibly strained knee and dodging through the crowd. Deciding that if she felt the pain in the morning, she would praise God for the glory of surviving this day, she focused on keeping up with Victor.

Without warning, he ducked into a recessed building entrance, spinning her so that her back pressed up against the brick wall. Through the arched entryway, she saw a man in black jeans and a black T-shirt run down the street, gun drawn, arms pumping. Her mouth went dry, and she lowered her head and closed her eyes, begging God for protection. When she opened her eyes again, she saw that one of her shoes had lost a heel. She slipped the other shoe off and used the brick wall as leverage to break the heel off. When she put it back on, it felt a little strange, but better than one heel on, one heel off.

"Hello, Mr. Kovalev." Frightened, Ruth spun around and saw two women, the brunette from the other day and a blonde, both in tight miniskirts and teetering platform heels descending the steps of the building. "We just got a call about you."

"Nina," Victor gasped. "I need to get out of the territory." He put his hands on his knees and bent over at the waist. Sweat dripped down his forehead. When he straightened, he shrugged out of his suit jacket and folded it over his arm. With his back to the brick archway, he glanced back down the street.

"You'll never get out," Nina whispered in a heavy

Russian accent. "Boris put a bounty on you. Whoever finds you, she is free to go."

He walked up to her and put a hand on her shoulder. "When I finish my testimony, everyone is free to go," Victor clarified. "Use your network. Get me out of here."

She glared at him as she shrugged away and adjusted her purse strap. "One time, one of the girls ran away. Boris brought all of us to one of your gyms and asked where she was. When we didn't speak up quick enough, he grabbed one of the girls and put her in the boxing ring with Vyacheslav Markoff." She spat on the ground as she said his name. "Vy beat her until she died while we all watched."

Ruth gasped, and Nina smiled at her. "And to think, all this happening every day around you and all of the other Americans in this city, and you get to say you never knew." Unable to meet her stare, Ruth looked down, and Nina continued.

"Boris told us he'd work through all of us until we told him where she'd gone. After I told him where she was, he had her beaten to death and left her on my couch." As she stepped out into the street, she turned and spoke to him in Russian before she walked out of sight.

Was she going to turn them in?

"What did she say?" Ruth asked, lifting her hair off her shoulders.

"That she'll never be free." He looked at the blonde woman, who dug through her purse then offered Ruth a rubber hairband. She felt tears sting her eyes at such a simple gesture.

"Thank you," she said as the girl walked to the archway and posed, leaning against the brick wall on the street side. "What are we going to do now?" she asked, quickly wrapping her hair into a bun high on her head.

"Nina will pull through. Give her two minutes." He looked at his watch. "Hopefully, the judge will postpone."

Ruth felt sick to her stomach at the plight of these girls, and so many like them. When despair started to descend over her, she reminded herself that the Kovalev Empire crumbling would free her and hundreds like her. Even if they died this morning, her testimony should put the father in prison. She knew the FBI had recorded Victor's interviews. She wondered if, in the event of the worst-case scenario, if the court could use those videos as evidence posthumously.

In the distance, she could hear sirens. "Should we go to the police?"

"Not until we're out of this neighborhood." The blonde girl reached in and tapped the wall behind her. He gestured with his head. "Here comes Nina."

She slipped into the alcove and pointed west. "Go. Watch for the girls' signals."

He smiled and kissed her cheek. "I owe you our lives, Nina. I won't forget that." Grabbing Ruth's hand, he said, "Let's go."

If she hadn't known a team of Russian prostitutes signaled him for the next three blocks, she would have never seen it. With subtle signs, they told him when to stop, when to turn around, and when the passage was safe. When a young black-haired girl held up a hand at a passing cab, Victor led her into a coffee shop and ducked behind the wall.

As Ruth craned to see the street, she saw a navy-blue SUV with Victor's gym logo emblazoned on the door slowly creep down the road. Instead of going back out the way they'd come in, they crossed over to the back and went out the back door into the alley. Like a few days before, they went into one building and out another, moving that way for a solid block. Finally, they stood right inside a bank's doorway, looking down the street at the courthouse.

Ruth instinctively knew that the moment they stepped out into the street and approached the courthouse, they would instantly have targets on their backs. Victor sighed and leaned his back against the wall. He reached up and gently touched her temple. "If you didn't look like a truck plowed into you, some of these bank employees wouldn't stare at us so obviously."

Now that they'd stopped moving her head hurt. In a bad way. So did her knee. She felt her temple with her hand and could feel the dried blood matting her hair. "We can't make it there on foot," she said, looking at her blouse and seeing the line of red that had clearly come from her head wound. She untucked her blouse and ripped a piece off the bottom of it, folding the cloth and pressing it to her temple, wincing a bit as she pressed against a bruise. "They'll be watching all entrances."

"I know." He looked at his watch. "Court would have started thirty minutes ago."

"Without you there, what will happen?"

He shook his head. "I have no idea. Hopefully, the

judge will just recess until they find out what's going on. The Marshal Service knows what happened. Marshal Brown contacted them as soon as we were hit."

"Excuse me, do you two have business here at the bank?" The security guard approached, looking at blood-covered Ruth suspiciously.

Victor smiled and placed his hand on the small of Ruth's back. "We were in an accident. Can I use your phone?"

"Accident? Where?"

Ruth gestured over her shoulder and lied. "A few blocks away. A bicycle messenger knocked me into the wall. I hit my head hard." She let her eyes fill with the tears she had forced at bay, and with one hand holding the cloth to her forehead, covered her stomach with another shaking hand. "I thought I could make it to the police station, but I started getting really dizzy."

A sympathetic look crossed the guard's face as he pulled a phone out of his pocket and handed it to Victor. "Come sit down over here," he insisted, leading her to a sitting area in between some desks. "Can I get you some water?"

With a shaking smile, Ruth nodded. "That would be wonderful. Thank you so much."

As Victor sat in the chair next to her and dialed a number, she gingerly prodded at her knee that had already started to swell up. "Marshal," Victor demanded, "where are you?" His face paled, and he immediately hung up the phone. "That was Boris."

Ruth's blood froze. Her throbbing knee forgotten for the moment, she straightened in the chair. "Now what?"

The guard returned with the water. Ruth wet the cloth and held it back up to the cut on her head.

Using the smartphone in his hand, Victor did an Internet search for the Federal Marshals' office. "I guess I'll just call the switchboard," he said. He held the phone up to his ear and raised his eyebrows when an operator answered. "My name is Victor Kovalev. I am currently with Doctor Ruth Burnette. We were attacked on our way to the courthouse and got separated from our detail." Ruth leaned over and put her ear up to the other side of the phone and heard the panicked operator ask him to hold the line.

Seconds later, someone answered. Victor gave him their location and hung up the phone. "Now we wait," he said.

The convoy of NYPD police officers and Federal Marshals escorting them the two blocks from the bank to the courthouse looked like a presidential detail. Despite the undeniable threat against their lives, Victor felt safe. He held Ruth's hand in his as they exited the Suburban and entered the courthouse, surrounded by law enforcement officers. Inside the doorway, Marshal Andrew Brown met them. "I thought they killed you!" Ruth said, shaking his free hand.

"They shot me in the vest. Anyway, when I went down, I lost my phone. Guess they found it." He shook hands with Victor. "Great job getting here. We were out looking for you."

He left them in a secure room to wait for the judge to

call the court to order. As they took their seats at the small round table, he studied Ruth. She had a dried trail of blood down the side of her face, and her ripped white silk blouse had black smudges and blood all over it. She'd pulled her hair back off her neck and wrapped it in a haphazard bun. Her freckles stood out dark against her pale face, and she had dark circles under her eyes. Even sitting here in the courthouse on a vinyl chair under fluorescent lights, she was the most beautiful woman he'd ever seen.

What she had endured for the last six months should have destroyed her. Instead, she still carried herself with the same grace and dignity that had attracted him to her in the first place.

He'd known when he met her that they could never truly be together. Personally, having nothing to do with his family's business dealings did not equate to ignorance of them, but through Ruth, he came to know Christ. What a beautiful gift God handed to him on his knees at the altar that Sunday. Redemption from sins, a love that came with no conditions, and a beautiful offer of grace that would sustain him through this earthly, oh-so-erred-human life. He couldn't believe he'd spent the first twenty-seven years of his life without the presence of God. And he fell hard for Ruth—beautiful, brilliant, loving Ruth. The longer he got to know her, the more time he spent with her, the more he convinced himself that he could find a way to separate from Antoly and Boris Kovalev and their nasty business and have a normal life.

When he lost Ruth, he felt like he'd lost everything.

He turned off a part of himself to go undercover. For six months, his father thought he finally had a son to make him feel proud and boastful. A boxing champion who, after retiring with the national title, finally took an interest in the family business. Instead, Victor made detailed logs, took notes, recorded conversations, and videoed everything he could using a high-tech camera that looked like a jacket button.

Going into it, he knew he would have to give up his life and go into witness protection. He would leave the courthouse today and disappear from New York forever, returning only to testify at various trials. He had already told his mother goodbye, but he wondered if he would have it in him to tell Ruth goodbye at the end of this day. Only the certain knowledge that Boris would hunt him down for the rest of his life kept him from falling to his knees and begging Ruth to marry him and go away with him.

A cell phone vibration broke his thoughts. He watched the agent at the door respond to a text then look at him. "Court is about to reconvene."

Ruth remained sitting. "I'd rather stay here," she said. "If they want to call me again, they can come get me here, right?"

Victor stopped at her chair and knelt down. Her eyes had a bit of a panicky look to them. "He won't be able to get to you in a crowded courtroom."

Her smile did nothing to take the skittish look out of her eyes. "I'm not willing to trust that."

Wondering if his familiarity with Nina and her friends had anything to do with this sudden desire to not be by his side, he put a hand over hers. "Ruth—"

"Good luck in there. I will wait here, and I will be praying for you." She put a hand on his shoulder and leaned forward, brushing her lips over his cheek. He closed his eyes, breathing in the smell of her, savoring the feel of her. "They're bringing me a medical bag so I can patch myself up."

Standing, he winked down at her. "I'll need the prayers." He smiled, then straightened his tie and followed the agent out of the room.

Chapter 13

"Mr. Kovalev, can you please tell us what happened on the night of December twenty-ninth of last year?" Darren Harris, the lead prosecutor, didn't waste any time. He jumped right into the questioning.

Victor looked at his father. The older man met his gaze with a steady stare, then finally gave a tiny, almost imperceptible nod. Even now, he clearly didn't understand Victor's intentions. He had spent hours receiving instructions and coaching from his father, uncle, and their attorneys. He had a script to follow, and Antoly believed his obedient son would follow it. Looking away from the cold stare of the man who had fathered him, he focused on Mr. Mitchell, who stood perfectly still near the table where he had papers and books stacked, waiting for Victor to speak.

He cleared his throat. "I had spent the evening training for a big fight that was scheduled for New Year's Eve." He turned his head and looked at the judge. "I used to professionally box and had a championship match at

Madison Square Garden that night." Looking back at Mr. Mitchell, he said, "But I'd had a concussion a couple of weeks before. That night in December, I was sparring with another fighter. He hit me in the side of the head, and even with the helmet on, I got really dizzy and weak. My trainer, Joe, sent me to his office to rest."

Mr. Harris walked up to the podium that stood between the two tables. He carried a single sheet of paper. "Why didn't you go home?"

"I live alone. I was really dizzy and really nauseated. Joe didn't want me alone. He planned to look in on me later in the night and decide if I needed to go to the hospital."

Mr. Harris nodded. "Go on, Mr. Kovalev."

"I barely made it to the back office. I laid down on the couch, and the next thing I knew, I'd been out for about two hours. My head hurt. I was sure I needed to go to the hospital, and I couldn't figure out why Joe had left me there."

He paused. At this point, his father would know he had veered off the assigned script. He kept his gaze trained on Mr. Harris, who nodded and asked, "What happened next?"

"I heard a man's pleading voice. I sat there on the couch and tried to make out the words, but I could barely hear him. Then I heard a gunshot. I went to the window, and by the time I got there, I'd heard two more shots. I looked out the window and saw my father standing in front of three bodies."

Antoly slapped his hand on the table in front of him. Victor paused, and Mr. Harris nodded at him. "Go on."

"As I started to leave, I ran into my father and one of his employees, Vyacheslav Markoff." He testified to the conversation he'd had with his father, and when he got to the part about Antoly putting the barrel of his gun to his forehead, he heard someone in the juror box gasp. In his peripheral vision, he saw his father whisper to his attorney. "He told me that he should kill me right there because my girlfriend had just threatened his empire. But instead of killing me, he would kill her. He said he looked forward to my suffering."

"Objection!"

Victor glanced at the judge, who looked at the attorney over the rims of his glasses. "Exactly what are you objecting to, Ms. Bynes?"

"Your honor, Antoly Kovalev is not on trial for the attempted murder of Ruth Burnette—"

The judge sighed. Victor watched him war with himself over what he would say next. Finally, quietly, he said, "Sustained." He looked at Mr. Harris. "Please contain your questions to this particular matter and this particular trial. I feel sure we'll have an opportunity to hear about this another time."

"Your honor—"

He waved a hand in the direction of Ms. Bynes. "Strike that last statement. Jury will disregard testimony regarding the attempted murder of Doctor Burnette."

Victor knew that he had used the element of surprise as the catalyst to get him this far in the questioning. From this point forward, the defense attorneys would stay on their toes and would barely allow him to speak a word. The prosecutor had prepared him for that.

Mentally backtracking to this case, he looked at Mr. Harris and waited for the question. "Can you tell us what you saw that night?"

Since he wasn't sure which of his many interviews Harris had pulled this question from, he thought it best to ask for clarity. "Can you be more specific?"

"From the time you woke up in your trainer's office until the time you left the gym, what did you see?"

As if someone had dinged a bell above his head, he felt his eyes widen as he nodded. "Initially, I only saw my father, Antoly Kovalev, with two of his lieutenants, Vyacheslav Markoff and Lev Genrich. Joe was gone, and the other boxers were gone. Then my father's cleanup agent arrived. His name is Mr. Kester. I've never known his first name, and I still don't."

Mr. Harris raised his eyebrow. "Can you explain what a cleanup agent is?"

Victor thought back to the tall, thin man with the cropped blond hair and empty, gray eyes. "His primary job for my father is to dispose of dead bodies and clean crime scenes, making sure no evidence remained that could be used to convict him."

"Objection!"

The judge looked at Victor. "I'm going to assume that you have more than just this."

"Yes, sir."

"Very well. Overruled."

"Your honor—"

"You know better, Ms. Bynes. Overruled." He gestured at Mr. Harris while he made a note on the book in front of him. "Continue."

"So, Mr. Kester arrived in the gym. How do you know why he was there?"

Feeling his stomach turn at the hours he spent in the company of Mr. Kester that night, he said quietly, "Because my father ordered me to assist Mr. Kester that night."

"Your honor! Hearsay!"

"Ms. Bynes. Sit down and close your mouth. The court will hear what the witness has to say. Prosecutor? Proceed."

"Thank you, your honor." Harris cleared his throat. "Assist with what?"

"While my father dispatched men to kill Ruth Burnette, I was ordered to help Mr. Kester dispose of the three men my father had ordered killed earlier that night. Their dead bodies were in the alley behind the gym." He looked directly at his father when he spoke the next words. No one murmured. No one shifted in their seats. Dead silence greeted him as he met his father's cold gaze. "The choice he gave me was to help Kester or give him four bodies to clean up instead of three."

Immediately, a sudden commotion broke out in the courtroom as people reacted to that statement. Antoly surged to his feet and screamed at Victor in Russian. "You are dead to me!" As his attorneys held him back and compelled him back into his seat, Victor looked at Mr. Harris and waited for the next question. "Dead! You hear me?"

When the door opened, Ruth looked up from writing in her notebook and watched Victor come into the room.

He looked tired, his face drawn, his mouth grim. He'd taken off his jacket and loosened his tie. She could see the dirt and bloodstains on his white shirt and wondered if he'd kept his jacket on during his testimony. When he saw her sitting at the table, his eyes widened in shock.

"You look surprised to see me," she said.

He pulled the chair next to her out from under the table and turned it around, sitting down and kicking his feet out in front of him. She closed the notebook and capped her pen. "I am surprised," he said, scooting down in the chair and leaning his head back until it touched the table. "When you didn't go into the courtroom with me, I thought you might go ahead and leave."

She pressed her lips together and nodded. "I thought about it. I have lived on this high alert for so many months, and then that ambush happened on the way to the courthouse. All I could think was that Boris was going to get me if I was with you."

"You're probably right." He rolled his head to look at her and took her hand in his. His scarred and swollen knuckles marked his years in the boxing ring. Bringing his hands to her lips, she kissed his knuckles and pressed them to her cheek.

"So, while you've been out there, baring your neck, I've been in here thinking about it and praying about it. And I've come to a conclusion."

"What would that be?" His voice had taken on a tired, husky edge.

With a deep breath, she closed her eyes and did a quick inner check, making sure she really meant what she intended to say. "I don't think that matters to me."

As she opened her eyes, she could see the intensity of his stare.

"Ruth, I knew what my family was when I asked you out. I had no business putting you and Esther at risk that way. I selfishly ignored that." He let go of her hand and straightened in the chair, scrubbing his face in his hands. "Now look at us," he said, gesturing at the room. "Your sister is murdered. You're on the run, and I even destroyed any chance of you returning to your pastor boyfriend and that little Florida town. It's all my fault."

Ruth cocked her head to look at him, trying to study him from every angle possible. For the last several hours, she had pondered questions deep in her heart. Could she separate him from Antoly? From Boris? From the crimes of his family? In the end, she knew she could. The Holy Spirit lived inside of him, and He created the wall that set Victor apart, that sanctified him. With the power of Almighty God behind him, he would overcome his upbringing. His strength and courage while working undercover for the last six months impressed her in ways she didn't know could impress her. She felt proud of him as if she had a right to claim pride where Victor was concerned.

"He wasn't my boyfriend," she replied. His eyebrow raised, but he didn't reply. She thought of Pastor Ben Carmichael and how much she admired him. "He was a good friend when I needed a good friend. He helped me a lot. He would have loved for me to return his feelings, but I just couldn't. I was too heartbroken over losing you to even consider ever loving another man again."

He stared at her, his eyes boring into hers. After

several long moments, he said, "And now?"

Hot tears suddenly burned her eyes. "And now you've said we can't be together because Boris is going to be after you." She reached for his hand, gripping it to express her urgency. "I don't care. He blames me, too. He knows if you hadn't ever fallen in love with me, that you'd have just maintained the even keel you were on. I'd rather be hiding and looking over my shoulder with you than without you."

"I don't think you understand what you're saying," Victor said urgently.

"For six months, I was completely on my own. Major was my only defense. And today, running down the streets of New York, with bullets pinging the cars all around us, I felt safer than I ever had because you had a hold of my hand."

"How can you say this? When you know who I am? You know where I'm from."

"I know who redeemed you, too." She stood up and lifted her palms, bringing her arms out on either side. "You get the same fresh start I got when I accepted Christ. You are a new creation, and the old you is dead. Don't you remember that part?"

Standing, he pulled her close, wrapping his arms around her. "Nothing about it will be easy," he said, his voice harsh.

"In Christ, we can do all things," Ruth said, smiling up at him.

Back when I first started this job," Marshal Dean Tucker said, hours after Victor concluded his testimony and endured the rigors of cross-examination, "distance was our greatest weapon. I could relocate someone from New York to Liberty, Kentucky, where no one knew them, and no one would likely cross their paths. Those were simpler times." He took a sip out of the blue coffee cup emblazoned with a gold Federal Marshal logo. "Right now, I'm battling 24-hour international media coverage and facial recognition software. I have gangs that are as well-equipped as some small countries with basically limitless online resources if you have someone who knows how to tap into them." He paused and met Victor's eyes. "Someone like your cousin Marco."

Ruth watched Victor's face. He grew very serious, very grim. She looked back at Marshal Tucker. "So, what can we do?"

"I see two choices before us." He pulled two file folders from his leather portfolio but kept them closed. Putting his finger on top of one, he said, "You can go to a tropical island somewhere where the Kovalev trial never touched. We'll set you up renting surfboards to tourists or something equally benign and safe, and you two can raise tanned children who become master sandcastle builders but who won't know a laptop from a coconut."

Despite the seriousness of the conversation, Ruth chuckled. Victor nodded toward the folders. "And door number two?"

Instead of answering directly, Marshal Tucker said, "Doctor Burnette, you've expressed a desire to return to your medical residency. We can do so, and we'll get your school transcripts and all that fixed so that you can, but one of the problems with that field is, again, the media and the publicity you'll require. Hospitals will want to post pictures. Articles you write will have pictures. You save a kid from a snakebite, and someone will take a picture, and so forth."

He took another sip of coffee and placed a finger on the second file folder. "You can say no, but I would recommend elective cosmetic surgery that would alter your appearance enough to fool digital facial recognition. For both of you. Then you two should be free to live your lives without fear."

Ruth thought about what that type of surgery would mean, the trauma for her body, the pain she'd have to endure. All were temporary things from which she could heal. It would also give her a sense of security and allow her to get back to work in the profession she loved. She looked at Victor, who squeezed her hand in support and nodded. "Okay," she agreed. Taking a deep breath, she said, "I'll do it."

"We'll both do it," Victor said.

Marshal Tucker nodded. He looked at his vibrating phone. "I'll get arrangements made. In the meantime, the judge is ready to marry you now. Mazeltov. Let's go."

Chapter 14

"Great surgery, Doctor Clark. Definitely one for the books." Ruth felt tired. They'd almost lost that patient on the table three times, but in the end, the team of surgeons won, and the patient currently lay in recovery. She looked forward to seeing her patient in the morning during rounds.

Ruth slipped the bandanna off her head as she pushed through the doors of the operating room, rolling her neck on her shoulders. "I am thrilled that we saved her. Thank you for the hand." Her phone vibrated in her pocket. "That must be Isaac."

She didn't think of herself as Ruth anymore. No one ever called her by her old name, including her husband. Her name, for the last three years, was Esther Clark. She answered with a smile and waved at the anesthesiologist who turned in another direction in the hall. "Hi there."

Victor's voice came over the line. "Coals should be hot soon. Should I put the steaks on?"

Her stomach growled at the thought. "Definitely.

Give me about thirty minutes, and I'll head that way."

After checking on her patients in the cardiac ICU, she updated charts, signing her three-year-old name, Esther Clark, so smoothly that a casual observer would suppose she had signed that name her entire life. Then she went to the locker room to change out of her scrubs. She paused when she looked at her reflection in the mirror on her locker door. The ever so slight changes made to her eyes, nose, and the shape of her mouth completely altered the way she looked. Sometimes it startled her. Because of her complexion, she couldn't do much to change the color of her hair, but she did cut it short, so it fell in sharp lines against her cheeks, straightened it, and added bold highlights to it.

She'd gotten used to the way Victor looked now. He looked far less Slavic. Sometimes, she missed his old chin. Other times, she could hardly remember what he'd looked like before.

She stepped out into the humid air of the South Carolina coastal town. After her time in Florida, she'd vied for another Florida placement. Because of the trial's publicity on the heels of the publicity of her saving the teenager, the Marshals turned her down flat. The closest they allowed was South Carolina. She'd suffered through a colder winter than she'd wanted, but as June gave way to July, she found she loved the hot, humid summers here as much as she had in Florida.

"Good night, doctor!" She looked up and waved at one of the nurses who had assisted in the surgery.

Digging through the pocket of her jeans, she pulled out her key fob and remotely unlocked her car. Out of cautious habit, she remotely locked it and unlocked it twice. Then, she hit the remote start function. As usual, the car didn't explode. At least now that the sun had gone down, the heat wouldn't suffocate her, and the car seat wouldn't sear the backs of her legs when she got in the car.

As she opened the door, something wrapped around her neck. Startled, she reached up and felt a man's arm. Her key fob got ripped from her grasping fingers before she could activate the panic button or use it as a weapon. "Hello, Doctor Burnette," a heavily accented voice growled in her ear. "I've been looking for you for such a long time now."

She felt the prick of what must have been a needle going into her neck, and almost immediately, her world went gray, then black.

Victor, now known as Isaac Clark, checked his watch for the tenth time in ten minutes. She should have gotten home over an hour ago. If a patient had caused the delay, she would have texted. In their three years of marriage, she always called or texted when she was delayed.

He looked at Major, who sat at the window, his ears up, straining to hear. Major whined and chuffed. "I know, boy. I'm worried, too."

He almost dropped his phone when it rang, her face flashing on the screen. "What happened?" he asked immediately.

"Your wife is the guest of honor at our family reunion," the voice on the other end said in Russian. He recognized his uncle Boris Kovalev's voice.

His blood froze in his veins, and he felt his hand tighten on the phone. "Where—?"

"Shut your mouth, or I'll go ahead and kill her right now." Victor clenched his teeth and took a deep breath through his nose. He could feel his heartbeat pulsing in a vein in his neck as his blood pressure spiked. After a few seconds, Boris said, "That's better. You can meet me. We'll spar. It will be just like old times." As he started to hang up the phone, he heard Boris's voice again. "Oh, and don't call your Marshal friends. Marco cloned your phone. I know what calls you make and receive. You call them? I take my time when I kill her."

Major jumped up and pranced to the door when he grabbed his car keys. Should he take him along? No. No distractions. "Stay," Victor commanded.

The dog whined but dejectedly walked back to his bed and lowered himself onto the cushion. He looked like he was ready to spring up at a second's notice, though. Outside, Victor got into his truck and started the engine. Where to? What did Boris mean by spar? He no longer boxed. He taught gym at the local high school. Could Boris be in the high school? Deciding to head in that direction, he turned left at the next intersection.

Five minutes later, he idled outside on the side of the road near the high school's back parking lot. At the entrance to the building that housed the basketball court, he saw a black sedan pulled up to the curb. He immediately knew Boris and Ruth waited inside for him. He sat there for five full minutes but saw no movement anywhere around the building. Did that mean that Boris hadn't put a lookout on duty, or was he just well hidden?

Overtly conscious of the ticking of the clock, he finally got out of his truck. Keeping as much in the shadows as possible, he ran across the parking lot, over the lawn of the school, and to the door closest to the faculty lounge. As quietly as possible, he unlocked the heavy metal door with his key. He slipped inside, bracing the door so it would shut without a sound. He paused, listening, waiting. Hearing no sounds, no approaching footsteps, no voices, he ran down the hall to the teacher's lounge, his athletic shoes making no sound on the polished tile floor.

Mr. Lewis, the Algebra teacher, kept a cell phone in his locker. He said parents always asked for his cell phone number, and he finally got one that he used for contacting parents. Leaving it at school instead of taking it home made it a joke to him. His arrogance, though, created a perfect opportunity for Victor. He cracked open Lewis' locker and pulled out the cell phone, using it to shoot Marshal Dean Tucker a text.

Boris found us. My high school.
He has her.

That small message would give the Marshal all the information he would need. Even though he worked out of an office three states away, he would dispatch law enforcement, and they would come in knowing that they dealt with a hostage situation.

After he left the lounge, he ran quietly along the hallways to the auto shop classroom. Once there, he found a hammer and screwdriver. He contemplated going to the Army JROTC wing, but he knew the weapons room had an alarm on it. While he wouldn't mind summoning police by breaking into it, he didn't know if the alarm would blare out through the school, and he had no desire to notify his uncle that he'd tried to steal a rifle from the rifle team supply.

Armed with just a hammer and screwdriver, he left the shop area and silently sprinted to the main entrance. Looking all around and seeing no one, he opened that door and let it shut loudly, allowing the metal clanging against metal to echo through the empty halls and announce his arrival. Quietly, he cracked the door open again and used a floor mat to prop the door open, hoping the police would arrive soon—not wanting them delayed with the need to figure out a way inside.

Ruth gradually opened her eyes. Mind foggy, unable to think, she struggled for a minute and discovered she couldn't move her hands or her arms. As she became more aware, she felt the ache in her shoulders. When she tried to shift them, she realized that someone had tied her hands above her head. Confused and startled, she blinked, forcing her eyes open. Boris Kovalev stood in front of her, grinning at her, his gold tooth shining in the dim light.

The gag in her mouth muffled her startled cry. When she jerked backward, she finally realized that Boris must have suspended her from the ceiling. After swinging for a moment, she found she could stand on her tiptoes to stop the momentum and relieve the pressure on her arms. Bracing herself on her booted toe, she closed her eyes and assessed the situation. Boris had found them, he'd drugged her with something that made her brain feel like he'd stuffed it with cotton balls, and he hadn't killed her yet. That could only mean that Victor was still alive, too.

More focused, calmer, she opened her eyes again. Boris laughed. "Glad you could join us. I worried I might have given you too big of a dose. Accidentally killed you before I was ready."

Looking up, head pounding, she recognized the ceiling of the high school gym. Her neck ached, and vertigo assaulted her. Straightening her head again, she battled against nausea that swirled in her stomach. Her mouth felt impossibly dry around the gag. As she fought the impulse to be sick, she felt a cold sweat break out on her forehead.

"Don't worry," a man laughed. Ruth did her best to crane her head around and recognized, Marco. "Victor is here to save you." He turned to his father and spoke in Russian. He walked toward her and put his nose next to hers. "He's a good husband, isn't he?"

She closed her eyes in pure defense against the manic evil she saw in his eyes. Silently, she began praying for her husband, praying that God would shield him from these men so bent on his destruction. Not caring about what happened to her, she just prayed he came out of there unscathed. Feeling a sob welling up in her chest, she tried to swallow it down. She would not give the Kovalevs the satisfaction of knowing the depths of her fear.

Chapter 15

Victor entered the gym, not knowing what to expect, feeling his feet falter when he saw Ruth suspended by her wrists from the ceiling. Her eyes were closed, but he knew she was conscious because he could see her leg muscles flex as she stood on her toes.

Rage surged through him at the sight of Marco sitting on a plastic chair looking at the screen of a laptop that sat propped on the bleacher. He quelled the desire to rip his cousin's throat out by first fisting his hands and taking a deep breath, then slowly releasing the air from his lungs and loosening his fingers. Rage would get them both killed. He had to think, be smarter, and faster than them.

Marco punched a few keys and lit a cigarette. Boris sat in a plastic chair, fingers steepled, eyes closed, looking like a man peacefully meditating.

At the sound of Victor's sneaker squeak on the polished floor, his eyes shot open. "Well, looks like we found the prodigal," Boris announced.

"I've contacted the Marshals. No matter what you do, you won't get out of this building a free man," Victor announced, his eyes on his wife. He watched as her eyes shot open at the sound of his voice. He could see the fear in her eyes. He wanted to run to her and reassure her that everything would be okay, but he couldn't. First, he had to contend with the darkness of his past.

Boris glanced at his son, who shook his head. "You're a liar," he said, standing. "I told you. Marco had your phone cloned. There's no way you were able to call them."

Victor shrugged. "That was my father's biggest problem with you, Boris, and why you never would have succeeded as the boss. You are narrow-minded and unable to see beyond your own shadowed and limited perception." He pulled the borrowed cell phone out of his pocket and tossed it to Marco. "My cell phone is not the only phone in this city I can use. There are phones, computers, tablets—any number of devices I could have used to silently send the Federal Marshals a signal."

Without warning, Boris surged to his feet, the chair sliding across the floor behind him. He picked up the baseball bat that had been at his feet and ran at Ruth, pulling back and swinging with all his might. The sound of the wooden bat cracking her ribs echoed through the gymnasium. Even through the gag in her mouth, Victor could hear her scream as tears poured out of her eyes. She looked at the ceiling and closed her eyes, her feet going limp, causing her arms to take the weight of her body. Without thinking about it, Victor dashed forward, tackling Boris and launching him to the ground. He blocked a blow from the bat just before Boris hit him in the temple with it, catching the full force of the blow with his forearm. Though his uncle outweighed him by a good sixty pounds, he had the advantage of youth and the reflexes of a professional boxer. He soon gained the upper hand. Sitting on top of his uncle, he used the handle of the hammer to apply pressure to his neck. His uncle's face turned purple, and his eyes bugged out. Victor continued to press. He didn't release the pressure, and his vision turned red with rage. All he could think about was destroying this man who had destroyed so many lives before him.

His wife's muffled screams preceded the sound of the gunshot by seconds. He felt the bullet enter his back and almost immediately lost the strength in his arms. He rolled off his uncle, putting his hand to his burning side, feeling the blood soaking his shirt. He'd spent most of his life in training, though, learning to fight through the pain, to embrace it, to use it to his advantage in a fight. With a roar, he launched from his knees toward his cousin, swinging with the hammer as he lunged at him.

Clearly thinking the mere presence of the gun would keep him in line, Marco did not react fast enough to defend against the attack. Victor swung the hammer as he surged to his feet, hitting his cousin in the cheekbone. Marco's head flew back with a sickening crack, and he collapsed at Victor's feet. With his hand gripping his side, Victor bent down and reached for the pistol. His hand fumbled and slipped on the wooden handle. Finally, he gripped it and raised it just as Marco got to his feet and rushed toward him. Firing twice, Victor watched as his cousin fell to the ground, his eyes staring unblinking at the ceiling. The expended brass cartridges rang against the hardwood gym floor like little choir bells, a sound that fell on his ears in an ironically cheerful way.

Boris made his way to his hands and knees. "I will kill you both," he rasped, a stream of spittle flying out of his mouth. "You will beg me for your life before you die."

Losing a lot of blood, Victor felt like the only recourse he had was to incapacitate his uncle. "You'll be in prison for the rest of your life," he said as he brought the butt of the pistol down hard on the man's head. His uncle's body jerked, then he slumped forward, his face hitting the ground. Victor stumbled over to Ruth and pulled the gag out of her mouth.

"Oh, thank you, God," she whispered.

Putting a bloody hand on her cheek, he kissed her seconds before he fell to the ground, unable to find the strength to untie his wife. Helpless, limbs not obeying the screaming in his mind to move, to help her, he stared at her panicked face as his eyes fluttered closed.

Ruth lay on the emergency room bed. She knew the doctor wanted to keep her overnight. Since Victor would likely not get out of surgery for another couple of hours, she didn't mind. She'd sent a friend home to take care of Major for her. Now she lay completely still, willing her broken ribs to heal superhumanly fast so she wouldn't be hindered when her husband came out of recovery.

She looked toward the door as Marshal Dean Tucker

came into her room. "Hello, Esther."

"How did he find us?" she asked by way of greeting.

"We found the body of your plastic surgeon this afternoon. It looks like Marco Kovalev hacked the doctor's computer and found the pictures of you the doctor had taken after your surgery. He then searched hospital databases until he matched your face."

Ruth felt a tear slip out of the corner of her eye. "Will we have to leave here?"

The Marshal kept his face expressionless. "That's up to you. The doctors don't know if Boris will regain consciousness. He wasn't a well man before he suffered such a blow to the head, and he may not even be able to physically come out of it. The doctors have given him about a thirty percent chance of living through the night. His son is dead. We have no idea if any other members of the Kovalev gang know where you are or even, at this point, if they care. Those that evaded arrest in the initial raids have not surfaced in three years."

Ruth frowned and thought about her father-in-law. "What about Antoly?"

"Antoly Kovalev suffered a massive coronary in prison six months ago. He is an old, weak man who won't live much longer."

"Why didn't you tell us?"

He shrugged. "I tried, but Isaac told me he didn't care about news of his family unless it pertained to his mother or directly with your safety." Even now, in the relative privacy of this hospital room with their covers fully blown and with the Kovalev family itself being openly discussed, Marshal Tucker's professionalism and training prevented him from referring to his WITSEC charges by their actual names.

Ruth looked at the white blanket covering her legs and considered that information. Finally, she nodded. "I agree with that." She took a deep breath and winced at the pain that somehow pushed through the haze of pain medication she'd taken. "I cannot imagine going back to being Ruth and Victor again. I will need to talk about it and pray about it with my husband so we can make a decision. We really love this life, and I don't want to relocate again unless we have to."

With a nod, he said, "Fair enough. For now, I have plainclothes Marshals guarding you two. Until we ascertain that the threat is over, you two will have no end of our company in this hospital."

She smiled. "Thank you, Marshal Tucker. And thanks for getting to us so quickly tonight. I'm sure you saved my husband's life."

Epilogue

Ruth stood in the doorway and watched as Zhanna Kovalev changed little Ben's diaper. She sang a Russian folksong to him as she finished snapping his nightshirt then pulled him into her arms. When she turned and saw Ruth in the doorway, she smiled and said in her broken English, "Mama home."

When Antoly Kovalev died in prison, Boris turned state's witness. With his testimony, he managed to bring down the entire Kovalev empire on an international scale. Ruth and Victor were finally free -- free to reclaim their identities, and free to live without fear.

Zhanna lived with them in their Florida home, helping care for their children. They'd relocated to Gainesville. Ruth had contacted Ben, and they met him and his wife for lunch in a cafe near the hospital where Ruth worked. She felt such a relief in telling him the whole story, in having the opportunity to speak to him openly and honestly, even ten years later. The two couples had become good friends. They regularly visited each other and let their toddlers play while they worked on a shared ministry project.

Because of Victor's father's dealings with slavery and the sex trade, Ben had helped him and Zhanna set up a ministry to help those who had once been enslaved receive counseling and rebuild their lives. He had just begun his residency at the hospital's psychiatric ward and had future plans to widen the reach of the ministry while Zhanna took English classes and went back to school to become a family counselor.

When an arm wrapped around her waist, she jumped in surprise only seconds before her husband's scent reached her nose. She placed her palms on his forearm and leaned against his chest. Zhanna set Ben on the quilt on the ground and handed him his favorite little rubber dinosaur. Their little red-haired Zhanna, named for her grandmother, rushed toward them and threw her arms around Ruth's legs. She laughed and picked her up, burying her face in her daughter's curls.

As she did daily, Ruth thanked God for the way He had protected them, physically, spiritually, and emotionally, over the events of the last decade. She leaned back and rested her head against her husband's chest. "It still amazes me, what God did," she murmured.

"He had a plan all along," Victor replied. He kissed the side of her neck. "Without us, Forty-Twenty-Nine wouldn't be."

They named their ministry after Isaiah 40:29, which read, "He gives power to the weak, and to those who have no might, He increases strength." Her arms tightened around her daughter, and her eyes filled with tears at the sight of her precious son. At her weakest moment, God had given her the power to stand firm and stand up to the evil that tried to destroy her.

Sometimes, she had a hard time remembering living in fear, faithful Major at her side protecting her from forces he didn't really understand, providing her the only security that would allow her to sleep at night. Now, as she looked around her home, she thought of the love that filled it and the peace and contentment contained in the walls. They would teach their children that they had the power to change the world because God would be beside them, increasing their strength.

Victor let her go and stepped away. "I need to start the grill. Ben and company will be here soon." He tickled baby Zhanna, making her giggle and wiggle in her mother's arms. Ruth laughed at the joy their daughter exhibited. Victor cupped her cheek and gave her a long, sweet kiss. When he stepped away, he said, "I love you." He tapped Zhanna on the nose. "I love you, too, little girl. Want to help daddy cook fish?"

"Fish!" Zhanna yelled as she let Victor scoop her out of Ruth's arms.

Ruth watched them go out onto the patio, then walked into the room and lowered herself onto the floor next to little Ben and his grandma. He tossed the toy down and crawled into her lap, happily babbling in his baby talk.

The End

Personal Note

A Note from author Hallee Bridgeman...

I'm so happy and honored that you chose to read *On the Ropes*. My sincere prayer is that the story of my fictional Mara and Victor the real stories that inspired me to write this single novella deeply blessed you.

According to the UN, international organized criminal organizations dealing in human trafficking enjoy an estimated annual profit of more than seven billion US dollars. The Russian mafia, in particular, have a protected connection to the industry of trafficking in humans. I pray that this novella shined even a glimmer of light on this very real darkness.

This was a difficult subject to write about, and I am equally sure parts of the novella were difficult to read. But my heart knows that these difficulties are very small compared to the difficulties faced by the real-life victims.

Writing is often a solitary profession, but it doesn't have to be. It would mean the world to me if you shared your thoughts by leaving an honest review for this book.

I would love to know your thoughts about this story. I really would.

I personally read every single book review, positive or otherwise. I'm not exaggerating. Even if you write just a few sentences about your favorite and least favorite aspect of *On the Ropes*, I would sincerely appreciate knowing your opinions.

Hearing from you lifts me up and helps me prayerfully craft the next story. An honest review also helps other readers make informed decisions when they seek through the thousands of choices on the bookshelf looking for an exciting, suspenseful Christian book for themselves.

Please use the link, or even your smartphone and the QR code on this page, to leave an honest review and tell me what you liked or didn't like about the story. I would so love to hear from you.

www.halleebridgeman.com/ReviewOTR

May God richly bless you,

Hallee Bridgeman

Discussion Questions

Suggested discussion group questions for *On the Ropes*. Victor Kovalev knows exactly who and what his father is, yet he still pursues a relationship with Ruth.

1. Do you think he should have been honest with her from the beginning?

As Mara, Ruth is terrified all of the time--except when she is in the sanctity of her church.

2. Do you believe that God will genuinely grant us the peace that passes understanding, or do you think Ruth's peace was something she brought upon herself?

Ruth immediately went to the police station and told them everything, even knowing, instinctively, that it would put her at risk.

3. Do you think that if she had made a different decision, like appealing to Antoly Kovalev, she could have saved her sister's life? Even by saving her sister's life, do you think that would have been the best decision?

Victor tried proselytizing to his father only once, then never tried again.

4. Have you ever encountered someone who you honestly would never attempt to tell about Christ? Is there someone in your life that you believe will never be open to the Gospel?

Victor regularly utilizes his friendships with the prostitutes under his father's command.

5. Do you think he should have acted sooner than he did to try to save them? Why or why not?

Victor and Ruth both make the decision to alter their appearances and live a lie.

6. How is this different from "thou shalt not lie" of the commandments of God? How is it justified?

Story Recipes

Suggested luncheon menu to enjoy when hosting a group discussion for *On the Ropes*.

Those who followed my Hallee the Homemaker website know that one thing I am passionate about in life is selecting, cooking, and savoring good whole real food. A special luncheon just goes hand in hand with hospitality and ministry.

For those planning a discussion group about this book, I offer some humble suggestions to help your special luncheon conversation come off as a success.

Esther's "World Famous" Chicken Salad

In the guise of Mara Harrison, Ruth enjoys a chicken salad sandwich based on her late sister's recipe. The comfort and familiarity of this simple meal lulls Ruth into a false sense of security, and she momentarily drops her assumed persona in front of pastor Ben.

Ingredients

2 split (1 whole) chicken breasts, bone-in, skin-on (about
    1 1/2 pounds)
extra virgin olive oil (cold-pressed organic is best)
salt (Kosher or sea salt is best)
fresh ground black pepper
1 cup pecan halves
1/2 cup sliced celery
1/2 cup good mayonnaise
1/2 cup plain yogurt (or sour cream)
1 1/2 tsp chopped fresh tarragon leaves
1 cup purple grapes, cut in halves
Your favorite whole grain bread, sliced thick

Preparation

Cook the chicken and prep the salad fixings.

Preheat the oven to 350° degrees F (175° degrees C).

Place the chicken breasts, skin side up, on a baking
sheet and rub them with olive oil. Sprinkle generously
with salt and pepper.

Roast for 35 to 40 minutes, until the chicken is
cooked through to 170° degrees F (75° degrees C)
internal temperature.

Set aside until cool.

Meanwhile, roughly chop the pecans.

Finely dice the celery.

Finely chop tarragon leaves.

Slice grapes in half.

Directions

When the chicken is cool, pull meat from the bones with fingers or a fork, then slice and dice the chicken meat to about a 1/2-inch dice.

Mix together the mayonnaise, yogurt, 2 teaspoons salt, and 1/2 teaspoon pepper.

Fold in the celery and chopped tarragon leaves.

Toss with the chicken, pecans, and grapes.

Serve open face with fresh romaine leaves or on your favorite whole grain bread. The next recipe here is for a beautiful whole grain bread if you want to try your hand at that.

You can also serve this chicken salad inside pita bread as a pocket or in a tortilla roll as a tasty wrap. Substitute sprouts for lettuce on your sandwich for an unforgettable flavor.

DELICIOUS WHOLE GRAIN BREAD

Just as Ruth felt confident and at ease in the surgical room, Esther felt at home in the kitchen. Baking was one of her very favorite activities. She loved to fill her home with the aroma of fresh-baked cookies, cupcakes, loaves of bread, or rolls. What follows is her "go-to" bread recipe.

Ingredients

3 TBS honey (pure, raw, local honey is always best)

2 1/4 tsp dry yeast (1 packet)

3 cups flour

(NOTE: I use a combination of fresh ground hard red and hard white wheat. If you don't have a way to use fresh ground, use unbleached white)

1 cup milk

1 tsp salt (Kosher or Sea salt is best)

3 TBS butter

Preparation

Lightly grease a large bowl to use for rising the bread

Melt the butter

Warm milk to 120° degrees F (48° degrees C).

Directions

Mix 1 TBS honey with warm the warm milk. Add yeast. Let stand for 5 minutes.

Place 2 cups flour and salt in a large bowl. Blend until well mixed. If using your stand mixture, turn on to speed 2 and add the remaining honey and the milk/yeast mixture. Add the melted butter. (If mixing by hand, mix well)

Add remaining flour 1/2 cup at a time until the dough is no longer sticky. Knead with the stand mixer for 2 minutes, or knead by hand for 10 minutes.

Once the dough becomes smooth and elastic, put it

into a lightly greased bowl. Turn it once and cover with a light towel. Let it sit in a warm spot until it doubles in bulk. It will take about an hour.

Punch the dough down. Roll dough into a rectangle and roll up tightly. Pinch the ends and place in a greased loaf pan. Cover and let rise in a warm place until nearly double in size.

Bake at 400° degrees F (205° degrees C) for 15 minutes. Reduce the temperature to 350° degrees F (180° degrees C) and bake 20 to 30 minutes longer When you tap the loaf, if it sounds hollow, it's done.

Remove from pan and immediately place it on the cooling rack.

This recipe makes one good-sized loaf. You can double it or triple it with ease assuming you have bread pans and counter space. Its best served fresh.

Uncut loaves of bread keep fresh in a plastic bag in the breadbox for up to two days. After a few days, you can still toast it or make French toast or croutons.

HOMEMADE POTATO CHIPS

To pinch a few pennies while the sisters were financially strapped medical students, Esther and Ruth would often make their own homemade potato chips. One of the best aspects of making your own chips besides the money savings is that you can control all of the ingredients as well.

Ingredients

Potatoes (I use garden-fresh or organic)

oil (You can use any kind of oil—safflower, peanut, grapeseed—whatever your frying oil of preference is, use it. I used canola oil—please make sure your canola is organic to avoid GMOs.)

salt (Kosher or sea salt is best)

Preparation

Wash your potatoes really well. I leave the skin on.

Directions

Using the mandolin, slice your potatoes very thin. I'm sure there are people out there with the knife skills to do this without a mandolin. I'm not one of them. My thinnest mandolin setting is 1/8 inch.

Heat the oil to 375° degrees F (190° degrees C). Gently slide the sliced potatoes into the oil, one slice at a time.

The oil is going to immediately bubble all around the slice. As it cooks, it's going to curl up and start to crisp. Once it curls up, try to turn it over (some don't make it over. That's fine) and keep cooking until they start to brown.

Remove them from the oil and place on a paper towel. I immediately sprinkle them with sea salt. They are best served fresh and will start to go stale very quickly. You can store these in a tightly covered container.

You can recover the oil once it cools. I strain and recover my oil and keep it in a tightly covered container in the refrigerator marked "potatoes." This way, I can use the same oil several times before having to replace it.

DARK CHOCOLATE CHIP COOKIES

During residency, Esther often arrived home hours before Ruth due to the varied demands of their chosen professions. At least once a week, she would surprise her sister with a special treat.

Ingredients

1/2 cup unsalted butter, softened
1/2 cup extra virgin coconut oil
1 cup sugar
2/3 cup light brown sugar
2 large eggs
1/4 cup unsulphured molasses
1 TBS vanilla extract
3 cups plus 3 TBS flour
(NOTE: I use fresh ground soft white wheat. If you don't
    have access to fresh ground wheat, use unbleached
    white flour)
1 tsp baking soda
1/2 tsp salt (Kosher or sea salt is best)
2 cups dark chocolate chips (1 each 12-ounce bag)
1 cup chopped pecans or walnuts

Preparation

Preheat oven to 400° degrees F (200° degrees C)
Chop nuts

Directions

Cream the butter, coconut oil, and sugars. Add the eggs, molasses, and vanilla extract. Mix well.

Add the dry ingredients and mix just until blended. Stir in the chocolate chips and nuts.

Place the bowl in the refrigerator and allow it to cool for 1 hour.

Drop by heaping tablespoons onto cookie sheet 2-inches apart.

Bake at 400° degrees F (200° degrees C) until just light golden – about 8 to 10 minutes.

This recipe makes about 70 cookies.

More Books

Find the latest information and connect with Hallee at her website: www.halleebridgeman.com

FICTION BOOKS BY HALLEE:

The Jewel Series:
Book 1, Sapphire Ice
Book 2, Greater Than Rubies
Book 3, Emerald Fire
Book 4, Topaz Heat
Book 5, Christmas Diamond
Book 6, Christmas Star Sapphire
Book 7, Jade's Match
Book 8, Chasing Pearl

Standalone Romantic Suspense:
On the Ropes

The Red Blood and Bluegrass Series:
Black Belt, White Dress
Blizzard in the Bluegrass
Coming Soon
The Seven Year Glitch

The Dixon Brothers Series
Book 1, Courting Calla
Book 2, Valerie's Verdict
Coming Soon
Book 3, Alexandra's Appeal
Book 4, Daisy's Decision

Virtues and Valor Series:
Book 1, Temperance's Trial
Book 2, Homeland's Hope
Book 3, Charity's Code
Book 4, A Parcel for Prudence
Book 5, Grace's Ground War
Book 6, Mission of Mercy
Book 7, Flight of Faith
Book 8, Valor's Vigil

COOKBOOKS BY HALLEE:

Parody Cookbook Series:
Vol 1: Fifty Shades of Gravy, a Christian gets Saucy
Vol 2: The Walking Bread, the Bread Will Rise
Vol 3: Iron Skillet Man, the Stark Truth about Pepper & Pots
Vol 4: Hallee Crockpotter, and the Chamber of Sacred Ingredients

The Song of Suspense Series

A Melody for James

MELODY Mason and James Montgomery lead separate lives of discord until an unexpected meeting brings them to a sinister realization. Unbeknownst to them, dark forces have directed their lives from the shadows, orchestrating movements that  keep them in disharmony. Fire, loss, and bloodshed can't shake their faith in God to see them through as they face a percussive climax that will leave lives forever changed.

♫ ♫ ♫ ♫

An Aria for Nick

 **ARIA** Suarez remembers her first real kiss and Nick Williams, the blue-eyed boy who passionately delivered it before heading off to combat. The news of his death is just a footnote in a long war, and her lifelong dream to become a world-class pianist is shattered on the day of his funeral.

Years later, Aria inadvertently uncovers a sinister plot that threatens the very foundations of a nation. Now, stalked by assassins and on the run, her only hope of survival is in trusting her very life to a man who has been dead for years.

A Carol for Kent

BOBBY Kent's name is synonymous with modern Country Music, and he is no stranger to running from overzealous fans and paparazzo. But he has no idea how to protect his daughter and Carol, the mother of his only child, from a vicious and ruthless serial killer bent on their destruction.

♫ ♫ ♫ ♫

A Harmony for Steve

CHRISTIAN contemporary singing sensation, Harmony Harper, seeks solitude after winning her umpteenth award. She finds herself amid the kind of spiritual crisis that only prayer and fasting can cure. Steve Slayer, the world-renowned satanic acid rock icon, who has a reputation for trashing women as well as hotel rooms, stumbles into her private retreat on the very edge of death.

In ministering to Steve, Harmony finds that the Holy Spirit is ministering to her aching soul. The two leave the wilderness sharing a special bond, and their hearts are changed forever.

They expect rejection back in their professional worlds. What neither of them could foresee is the chain of ominous events that threaten their very lives.

♫ ♫ ♫ ♫

Available in eBook, Paperback, or Hardcover
wherever fine books are sold.

THE JEWEL SERIES

Book 1: Sapphire Ice

Robin's heart is as cold as her frosty blue eyes. After a terrifying childhood, she trusts neither God nor men. With kindness and faith, Tony prays for the opportunity to shatter the wall of ice around her heart.

Book 2: Greater Than Rubies

Robin plans a dream wedding. Anxiety arises when she realizes the massive changes marriage will bring.

Nightmares resurface reminding Robin of past horrors. Giving in to her insecurities, she cancels Boston's "Royal Wedding." With God's guidance, can her bridegroom show Robin her true worth?

Book 3: Emerald Fire

Green-eyed Maxine fights daily to extinguish the embers of her fiery youth. Barry's faith in God is deeply shaken when he is suddenly widowed. Just as they begin to live the "happily ever after" love story that neither of them ever dreamed could come true, a sudden and nightmarish catastrophe strikes that could wreck everything. Will her husband find peace and strength enough to carry them through the flames?

Book 4: Topaz Heat

Honey eyed Sarah remembers absolutely nothing from her bloodcurdling younger years. Derrick fled a young  life of crime to become a billionaire's successful protégé. After years of ignoring the heat between them, they surrender to love, but must truly live their faith to see them through.

Book 5: Christmas Diamond

Christmas Diamond begins the second-generation Jewel series by relating the tale of how a young British pilot named Faith Green stumbles upon TJ Viscolli, and how  their lives become intertwined from that very moment.

Book 6: Christmas Star Sapphire

Madeline Viscolli is doing her post-graduate studies in the Mobile Bay area of Alabama. Christmas is a time of family, but Joe Westcott has determined to stay alone and single. Madeline comes into his life and causes him to start reevaluating what he considers important. A Christmas Eve funeral brings everything to a crest, and Joe and Maddie are forced to make a choice that will affect their entire future.

Book 7: Jade's Match

Former Olympian Cora "Jade" Anderson and Olympic hopeful Davis Elliot live their romance very publicly through social media, but hate and racism threaten to destroy the relationship. Can the Olympians overcome the obstacles, or will they have to concede the match?

Book 8: Chasing Pearl

For Violet Pearl and Chase Anderson to end up together, one of them will have to make a huge move. A message from God arrives in the form of a package from 1940. This humble box brings their hearts together even though they live and work thousands of miles apart. Each must listen closely to the message to close the distance.

Available wherever fine books are sold.

About Hallee

With nearly a million sales, Hallee Bridgeman is a best-selling Christian author who writes romance and action-packed romantic suspense focusing on realistic characters who face real-world problems.

An Army brat turned Floridian, Hallee finally settled in central Kentucky with her family so she could enjoy the beautiful changing of the seasons. She enjoys the roller-coaster ride thrills that life delivers with a National Guard husband, a daughter away at college, and two middle-school-aged sons.

A prolific writer, when she's not penning novels, you will find her in the kitchen which she considers the "heart of the home." Her passion for cooking spurred her to launch a whole food, real food "Parody" cookbook series. In addition to dozens of nutritious, Biblically grounded recipes, each cookbook also confronts some controversial aspect of secular pop culture.

Hallee has served as the Director of the Kentucky Christian Writers Conference and continues to serve on the Executive board, President of the Faith-Hope-Love chapter of the Romance Writers of America, and board Secretary for Novelists, Inc. (NINC). She is a long time Gold member of the American Christian Fiction Writers (ACFW), and a member of the American Christian Writers (ACW). An accomplished speaker, Hallee has taught and inspired writers around the globe, from Sydney, Australia, to Dallas, Texas, to Portland, Oregon, to Washington, D.C., and all places in between.

Hallee loves coffee, campy action movies, and regular date nights with her husband. Above all else, she loves God with all of her heart, soul, mind, and strength; has been redeemed by the blood of Christ; and relies on the presence of the Holy Spirit to guide her. She prays her work here on earth is a blessing to you and would love to hear from you.

Sign up for Hallee's monthly newsletter! You will receive a link to download Hallee's romantic suspense novella, *On the Ropes*. Every newsletter recipient is automatically entered into a monthly giveaway! The real prize is never missing updates about upcoming releases, book signings, appearances, or other events.

Hallee Online

Newsletter Sign Up:
halleebridgeman.com/newsletter

Author Site:
www.halleebridgeman.com

Facebook:
facebook.com/authorhalleebridgeman

Twitter:
twitter.com/halleeb

Goodreads:
goodreads.com/author/show/5815249.Hallee_Bridgeman

Homemaking Blog:
www.halleethehomemaker.com

Blogger with **Inspy Romance** at
www.inspyromance.com

Newsletter

Sign up for Hallee's monthly newsletter! Every newsletter recipient is automatically entered into a monthly giveaway! The real prize is you will never miss updates about upcoming releases, book signings, appearances, or other events.

Hallee's Newsletter

halleebridgeman.com/newsletter

Made in the USA
Monee, IL
16 November 2022

17840803R00102